"You're not much of a liar, Maren Minnesota."

"I don't get much practice."

"That's good." The softly whispered words hung between them. "Honesty is a very sexy quality in a woman." Jared brushed a soft kiss against her hair. He felt his heart aching. He hated this tangled web.

"You make me want to do things, Maren." He framed her face in his hands, his heart speeding up and beating wildly in his chest. "Wild, insane things."

She could feel her breath backing up in her lungs. She wanted to believe him, believe in the moment, in what was happening between them, even as every sane bone in her body begged her to run for cover. But she wasn't listening to sanity, she was listening to the rush of desire as it overtook her.

"Such as?"

He didn't want words any longer.

He wanted her.

Dear Reader,

Welcome to the New Year—and to another month of fabulous reading. We've got a lineup of books you won't be able to resist, starting with the latest CAVANAUGH JUSTICE title from RITA® Award winner Marie Ferrarella. *Dangerous Disguise* takes an undercover hero, adds a tempting heroine, then mixes them up with a Mob money-laundering operation run out of a restaurant. It's a recipe for irresistibility.

Undercover Mistress is the latest STARRS OF THE WEST title from multi-RITA® Award-winning author Kathleen Creighton. A desperate rescue leads to an unlikely alliance between a soap opera actress who's nowhere near as ditsy as everyone assumes and a federal agent who's finally discovered he has a heart. In *Close to the Edge*, Kylie Brant takes a bayou-born private detective and his high-society boss, then forces them onto a case where "hands off" turns at last into "hands on." In Susan Vaughan's *Code Name: Fiancée*, when agent Vanessa Wade has to pose as the fiancée of wealthy Nick Markos, it's all for the sake of national security. Or is it? Desire writer Michelle Celmer joins the Intimate Moments roster with *Running on Empty*, an amnesia story that starts at the local discount store and ends up…in bed. Finally, Barbara Phinney makes her second appearance in the line with *Necessary Secrets*, introducing a pregnant heroine and a sexy cop—but everyone's got secrets to hide.

Enjoy them all, then come back next month for more of the best and most exciting romantic reading around.

Yours,

Leslie J. Wainger
Executive Editor

Please address questions and book requests to:
Silhouette Reader Service
U.S.: 3010 Walden Ave., P.O. Box 1325, Buffalo, NY 14269
Canadian: P.O. Box 609, Fort Erie, Ont. L2A 5X3

Dangerous Disguise

MARIE FERRARELLA

Silhouette®

INTIMATE MOMENTS™

Published by Silhouette Books

America's Publisher of Contemporary Romance

SILHOUETTE BOOKS

ISBN 0-373-27409-2

DANGEROUS DISGUISE

Copyright © 2005 by Marie Rydzynski-Ferrarella

Visit Silhouette Books at www.eHarlequin.com

Printed in U.S.A.

Books by Marie Ferrarella in Miniseries

ChildFinders, Inc.
A Hero for All Seasons IM #932
A Forever Kind of Hero IM #943
Hero in the Nick of Time IM #956
Hero for Hire IM #1042
An Uncommon Hero Silhouette Books
A Hero in Her Eyes IM #1059
Heart of a Hero IM #1105

Baby's Choice
Caution: Baby Ahead SR #1007
Mother on the Wing SR #1026
Baby Times Two SR #1037

The Baby of the Month Club
Baby's First Christmas SE #997
Happy New Year—Baby! IM #686
The 7lb., 2oz. Valentine Yours Truly
Husband: Optional SD #988
Do You Take This Child? SR #1145
Detective Dad World's Most
  Eligible Bachelors
The Once and Future Father IM #1017
In the Family Way Silhouette Books
Baby Talk Silhouette Books
An Abundance of Babies SE #1422

Like Mother, Like Daughter
One Plus One Makes Marriage SR #1328
Never Too Late for Love SR #1351

The Bachelors of Blair Memorial
In Graywolf's Hands IM #1155
M.D. Most Wanted IM #1167
Mac's Bedside Manner SE #1492
Undercover M.D. IM #1191
The M.D.'s Surprise Family. IM #1653

Two Halves of a Whole
The Baby Came C.O.D. SR #1264
Desperately Seeking Twin Yours Truly

*The Reeds
Callaghan's Way IM #601
Serena McKee's Back in Town IM #808

*Unflashed series

Those Sinclairs
Holding Out for a Hero IM #496
Heroes Great and Small IM #501
Christmas Every Day IM #538
Caitlin's Guardian Angel IM #661

The Cutlers of the Shady Lady Ranch
(Yours Truly titles)
Fiona and the Sexy Stranger
Cowboys Are for Loving
Will and the Headstrong Female
The Law and Ginny Marlow
A Match for Morgan
A Triple Threat to Bachelorhood SR #1564

*McClellans & Marinos
Man Trouble SR #815
The Taming of the Teen SR #839
Babies on His Mind SR #920
The Baby Beneath the Mistletoe SR #1408

*The Alaskans
Wife in the Mail SE #1217
Stand-In Mom SE #1294
Found: His Perfect Wife SE #1310
The M.D. Meets His Match SE #1401
Lily and the Lawman SE #1467
The Bride Wore Blue Jeans SE #1565

*The Pendletons
Baby in the Middle SE #892
Husband: Some Assembly Required SE #931

The Mom Squad
A Billionaire and a Baby SE #1528
A Bachelor and a Baby SD #1503
The Baby Mission IM #1220
Beauty and the Baby SR #1668

Cavanaugh Justice
Racing Against Time IM #1249
Crime and Passion IM #1256
Internal Affair Silhouette Books
Dangerous Games IM #1274
The Strong Silent Type SE #1613
Cavanaugh's Woman SE #1617
In Broad Daylight IM #1315
Alone in the Dark IM #1327
Dangerous Disguise IM #1339

MARIE FERRARELLA

This RITA® Award-winning author has written over one hundred and twenty books for Silhouette, some under the name Marie Nicole. Her romances are beloved by fans worldwide.

To
Mark.
Nothing is impossible,
as long as you
believe.

Chapter 1

He was too good-looking.

The thought telegraphed itself across Maren Minnesota's mind the moment she walked into her office.
Tucked away behind the kitchen, the small, windowless
room was crammed with not one desk, but two since she
shared the space with Joe Collins, the accountant for
both branches of Rainbow's End and the man she regarded, for all intents and purposes, as her father. Two
of the walls were lined with shelves that housed books,
knickknacks, and an antiquated stereo system.

The man sitting in the chair by her desk made the rest
of the room fade away.

She was running a few minutes behind, which was

unlike her. Maren had completely forgotten that she had an appointment to interview a Jared Stevens and that said Jared Stevens was waiting for her in the office. If it hadn't been for April, the salad girl, prompting her, who knew how long the man would have gone on waiting. He was interviewing for the position of assistant chef, a job that had suddenly become vacant.

As manager of Rainbow's End's main restaurant, she'd seen three candidates so far in the last two days and none had impressed her as particularly right for the job. She knew she was being too fussy. In her experience, it took a certain zest to cook creatively, a certain passion for food, a flair for color to make an outstanding chef. The other people she'd interviewed—two men and a woman—had résumés that were decent enough, but she didn't quite have the feeling that they could offer as much dedication as was needed.

It was her goal to make this particular branch of Rainbow's End the best.

But this man, who had brought over Papa Joe's chair and angled it beside her desk, well, she detected a little too much passion to suit her. More than likely, that passion wouldn't be strictly aimed at the vegetables and meat.

She knew this because her breath had caught in her throat when their eyes met. Jared Stevens had turned in his chair when she'd opened the door. His incredible green eyes made instant contact with hers, as if their meeting had been preordained somewhere in some vast eternal book.

If she had been a battleship, she would have immediately been sunk.

It took her half a second to recover.

He reminded her of Kirk. And that was a bad thing. A very bad thing.

Kirk Kendell had been almost mind-numbingly good-looking, too, with the same jet-black hair and green eyes, the same chiseled, sexy looks. That would have been the only way she could describe it. Mind-numbing. Because, during their relationship that occurred the last two years she was in college, her mind had certainly been numbed. Or, more accurately, missing in action. On the occasions that she allowed herself to look back, she silently referred to that time frame as her stupid period.

She didn't like being reminded of it.

Which gave Jared Stevens a very big strike against him.

"Is something wrong?" The deep voice filled the room and rolled over her like a warm desert wind. It made her think of chocolate, deep and rich.

Still standing in the doorway, she took a breath. Took control. She became the epitome of efficiency as she willed her legs to move. "No, why?"

He was smiling now and she felt her stomach lurch, then tighten. He had the kind of smile that whispered "seduction."

"Because you're staring," he told her as he rose to his feet.

At least he has manners, she thought.

Maren cleared her throat and walked into the room, purposely leaving the door open behind her. Air tended to become scarce in the small office at times and, right now, she needed all the air she could get.

She said the first thing that popped into her head. "Just trying to envision you in a chef's hat."

He looked surprised and somewhat bemused. One dark, perfectly shaped eyebrow raised itself higher than the other. "Then I have the job?"

"No, you don't." She did her best to sound professional and not curt. "I was just jumping ahead." It was a lie, but she wasn't at her most creative right then.

Taking her chair, she motioned for him to sit down again. Maren picked up the résumé on her desk. Although she'd already gone over it once, she scanned it again. The names of his previous employers were far from run-of-the-mill or average. Valentino's in New York and The Cattleman in Dallas. Both restaurants demanded perfection.

"Impressive," she commented. Normally gregarious and bent on putting people at their ease, she held herself in check. There wasn't an ounce of emotion evident in her voice. She raised her eyes to his. "You seem to move around a lot."

"Not a lot," he countered. She noticed no trace of a regional-defining accent in his voice. "Just New York City and Dallas. I always wanted to see them," he added in a tone that seemed unsettlingly intimate, as if he was sharing a secret with her. "And a man has to eat."

"That's what we're counting on," she responded in her most crisp, distant voice.

The open door wasn't helping. The air stood still today. His eyes looked as if he could see right into her thoughts, her sudden vulnerability.

She liked to think of herself as a confident woman. Despite everything that had happened in her life, or maybe because of it, she hung on to confidence as if it were a cloak. It shielded her from unsettling situations. She worked hard to make sure that nothing interfered with that confidence and sitting across from this man with the bedroom-green eyes made her feel anything but.

She wanted to have as little to do with men like Jared Stevens as humanly possible.

Outstanding résumé or not, hiring him as assistant chef wouldn't be wise. She wasn't given to agonizing over her decisions, but she wasn't prone to snap judgments, either. Except in this one sensitive area.

Maren made up her mind without bothering to call either of the two highly regarded restaurants he had listed, or the names he'd included under references.

He wasn't going to get the job.

She'd sooner go with the woman who had come in yesterday. The small, chatty blonde was fresh out of cooking school and eager. Eager could be molded and taught. She knew that firsthand. She'd been eager. Once.

Jared leaned over and broke the pregnant silence. "Would you like to give me a test run?"

Maren's head jerked up as surprise blossomed all through her. Was the man propositioning her in exchange for a job? "Excuse me?"

"In the kitchen." He nodded his dark head toward the area just beyond the office. "Would you like me to cook something for you? I can whip up anything you name."

Arrogant, just like Kirk.

Maren shored up her beaches. Turning someone down for a job was always done best swiftly, like ripping off a Band-Aid from a wound. Going slowly only prolonged everyone's agony.

"No, I don't think that's going to be necessary. I'm really sorry, Mr.—" Stumbling, Maren glanced at the top of the form again. "Mr. Stevens. But—"

She saw him open his mouth, undoubtedly to argue her out of her decision or perhaps to bargain his way into a trial period, but just then a blood-freezing shriek filled the air. Maren's eyes widened as she turned her head toward the source.

The shriek came from the kitchen.

Before she could gain her feet, the would-be chef whose interview she was terminating was dashing toward the origin of the sound.

Right behind him, she saw it the second she crossed the threshold into the kitchen.

Flames shot up from within one of the frying pans on the stove. The blaze looked ready to cut loose and spread throughout the kitchen in less than a heartbeat. Max, the head chef, April, the salad girl, and Rachel, one of the dessert chefs, were all backing away from the stove. April had been the one to scream, and she was still screaming.

Only Jared was moving toward the fire.

It was a grease fire, Maren realized. She saw the man who'd just been in her office, the man she'd been ready to send away, grab a cast-iron lid and quickly drop it on the pan.

"Fire extinguisher!" he yelled to her. "Where's your fire extinguisher?"

Rather than answer, Maren yanked it from the wall and rushed toward him. Jared grabbed the canister out of her hands and liberally sprayed directly at the flames that were trying to escape the pan. The sparks vanished, but he still sprayed all around the area. The fire was out in less time than it took to tell about it, leaving behind an awful smell that threatened to hang in the air for hours.

Jared switched on the two exhaust fans directly above the frying pan.

Lowering the now-empty canister, he glanced at Maren over his shoulder. "Is this what you call trial by fire?"

She could only shake her head. This could have really been a disaster. If it had gotten out of hand, at the very least, the fire could have forced them to close down for several weeks. Maren looked at the man with new eyes.

She wasn't being fair to him, condemning him because of his face.

"That was quick thinking. Thanks. Just put it down out of the way," she instructed when he offered to hand her the extinguisher. Max, April and Rachel had all come forward again, gathering around her. Relief was etched on each of their faces. Maren looked from one to the other. "What happened?"

Rachel, the oldest, looked somewhat chagrined. "I don't know, Maren. I was just preparing the sweet tarts and I must have knocked over the oil. The pan was still hot and..." Her voice trailed off as her thin shoulders rose and fell. "I'm sorry, Maren, I don't know how that oil got there. I know I didn't put it there myself—"

Maren raised her hand, waving away the apology before it made a reappearance. She wanted this behind them.

"That's all right, nothing happened," Maren said, her eyes shifting toward the man who had just possibly saved her from an incredible amount of inconvenience. Things could get out of hand quickly in a kitchen. "Thanks to Mr. Stevens."

There was that smile again, the one that could melt concrete, she thought. "Jared," Jared corrected.

Max looked him over. It was evident that the man regarded Jared as competition. "You the new guy?" he asked.

"I don't know." Green eyes turned toward Maren. "Am I?"

That uneasy feeling was still there, making her feel as if she were searching for a door that had been there a moment ago but had somehow disappeared. The feeling was not unlike the one generated by similar dreams she'd had. It made her leery.

But after what he'd just done, added to the résumé that sat on her desk, it didn't seem fair to turn him away. His only flaw was that he reminded her of someone she didn't want to remember.

Jared Stevens was too good-looking, she thought again. Good-looking men tended to wait for things to be handed to them. Like opportunities. And hearts. She was being childish. As well as unfair. And Maren had always believed in being fair.

She dragged her hand through dark blond hair the color of gold nuggets at sunset. "After what you just did, it wouldn't seem fair to turn you down without a trial run."

She saw him breathe a sigh of relief. It made her think that he really needed this job.

"That's all I ask, Ms. Minnesota." His smile widened. "A fair chance."

Something rippled through her. Maren looked away from her newest staff member. Unconsciously she ran her tongue along her lower lip. It was something she did when she was feeling less than confident about the wisdom of a decision. But she'd already hired him, albeit on a trial basis. His position was contingent on how well he lived up to the praise in his résumé and just as importantly, how well he melded with the staff. She prided herself on running a well-oiled machine.

"Can you start tomorrow?"

"Absolutely." Genuine enthusiasm throbbed in his voice and she felt a little better about her decision. Maybe this would work out in the long run.

Jared put his hand out to hers. After a beat, she took it, sealing the bargain.

He grinned at her, releasing her hand a bit slower than she thought he should have. "My dad always said you could tell a lot about a person by their handshake."

Said. She wondered if he was just using his words loosely, or if this meant that his father was deceased. At any rate, if the man was any more charming, she thought, charm would literally drip from his fingertips.

The specter of Kirk was difficult for her to shake. Kirk had been a charming manipulator, something she'd found out too late to save her heart.

She decided Jared Stevens was the kind of man who never truly "needed" anything. He got by on his looks and charm. And wits, she added, thinking of the fire he'd just averted. She supposed if he cooked as well as the résumé seemed to indicate he did, she could do a lot worse than having a man like him on the staff.

As long as he kept his distance.

But not for now. She looked back toward her office and straightened slightly. Business first, self-preservation later.

"Then come in, I have some papers for you to fill out and sign." She offered him a perfunctory smile that remained strictly on her lips and didn't reach her eyes.

"On behalf of Mr. Shepherd and Mr. Rineholdt, welcome to Rainbow's End." *At least for now,* she added silently as she led the way back into the office.

Half an hour later, his fingers cramping from the writing he'd just done, Jared got in behind the wheel of the slightly less than pristine electric-blue Mustang the department had him driving these days.

He breathed a sigh of relief, glad that was over. Women didn't generally prove to be an obstacle for him. But this boss lady hadn't been as easy as he'd thought she'd be, he thought as he started up his car. It coughed and then rumbled awake. He missed his sporty convertible, but that didn't go with the image he was trying to project. That of someone working his way up.

Backing out of the parking lot, Jared pointed his vehicle straight for his uncle's house. He had a lot to do before tomorrow.

It was a lucky break that the fire had begun when it had, otherwise he wasn't all that certain that the lady with the killer body and drop-dead long legs would have hired him. At least, not without a great deal more persuasion from him. She'd looked reluctant in her office before that girl had screamed. But then he'd always had more than his share of luck, he mused, turning up the sound on the radio. The station was playing a song he liked and he let the beat energize him.

The odd thing was, the reluctance Maren Minnesota had displayed seemed to have been immediate, before she'd looked at his credentials. She'd already seen his résumé, so her problem with him couldn't have been anything on the paper, otherwise she wouldn't have asked him to interview in the first place.

He wondered if she was naturally leery of strangers or if she was reacting to something specific about him. An amused smile played on his lips. His song was over, but he left the volume on high, letting the music surround him. Maybe the woman had a keen sixth sense when it came to undercover detectives, he mused. The idea no sooner came to him than he frowned. He sure as hell hoped that wasn't it. Anonymity was the name of the game.

But then, who knew how she figured into all of this. She could be the ringleader to the restaurant's criminal operation. Just because she looked melt-in-your-mouth delectable didn't mean she didn't have the brains of a master criminal. Being a woman had never gotten in the way of people like Catherine de Médicis and Lucrezia Borgia.

Everyone was a suspect until he sorted this latest assignment out.

Right now, he wanted one last brush-up lesson from his uncle. It never hurt to be too prepared when dealing with criminals.

He'd downloaded the Rainbow's End menu, both lunch and dinner, off the Internet last night. He'd familiarized himself with all the ingredients that went into preparing every dish. Overkill, maybe, but when his life might be on the line, it didn't hurt to wear suspenders and a belt.

To counterbalance that, his nature demanded that he take risks and play long shots, but never at the beginning of an assignment. Then he wanted to make sure all his ducks were in a row and swimming to the best of their ability.

After taking the freeway for one exit, Jared got off. Midday traffic was light in this part of town. His luck was holding.

Out of all the Cavanaughs, he supposed he was the best cook. Not counting Uncle Andrew, of course. Andrew Cavanaugh, former chief of the Aurora California police department and family patriarch, had put himself through school working as a short-order cook. After his wife Rose had disappeared over fifteen years ago, Andrew had taken over the duties of both parents. His cooking improved. And once he retired from the force, his talents continued to flourish.

Things hadn't changed when his wife was found last year, not in some shallow grave or in the river, the way everyone feared, but suffering from amnesia.

These days, Jared thought with a warm smile, his uncle and aunt sometimes competed for control of the kitchen. No one had the heart to tell Aunt Rose that Uncle Andrew could cook rings around her. But then, in his opinion, no one could hold a candle to Uncle Andrew.

He'd been taking lessons from Andrew these past

two weeks. Ever since this assignment had come to
light. At the time, the assistant chef at Rainbow's End
hadn't left his position yet. But the man had come to
the police department with very grave suspicions and
some very serious allegations.

What the man had to say had been heard and duly
noted. The chef had then been persuaded to take a leave
of absence from work citing a sudden "family emergency."

And he was the man the department had sent to fill
the vacancy, Jared thought as he drove past a strip mall
to the light. The other three applicants for the job had
been from the police force as well. His father, the current chief of detectives, Brian Cavanaugh, was taking
no chances. He was loading the deck, not wanting to
lose the opening that the department had arranged in the
first place.

The others were good, but he was better, Jared
thought with absolutely no conceit. He was born for this
kind of work. Making a right, he drove into his uncle's
development. There was no doubt about it. He had a
passion for undercover work, for never being the same
person twice. It turned each day into a challenge and he
liked challenges. They kept him on his toes, kept him
from getting stale.

Jared pulled up into the driveway of the house where
he'd had breakfast just a few hours ago. Making breakfast for not only his immediate family but his extended
one as well was a ritual his uncle had insisted on over

the past dozen years or so. Never more so than now when his own five children—all detectives on the Aurora Police Force—had left the "nest" to begin their own families.

No doubt about it, they were dropping like flies, Jared mused as he got out of the Mustang. His cousins, all seven of them, even his older brother Dax, had all succumbed to the lure of marriage.

But not him, he thought. Never him. Marriage wasn't something that had ever fit in with his plans, much less held any appeal for him. He liked meeting new women, being with new women.

Like that one he'd met today.

But he was getting ahead of himself. First the bust, then the rewards, if there were to be any.

Jared knocked on the back door and then tried the doorknob. As always, the door was unlocked. Jared walked into the kitchen, which somehow always managed to have warm, delicious smells permeating the air.

You'd think that the former chief of police would take a more aggressive stand toward safeguarding his house, Jared thought not for the first time.

"Uncle Andrew," he called out. "It's Jared. I thought maybe I'd squeeze in one last lesson unless you're too busy."

A man of average height and in his fifties, still in very good shape for his age, appeared almost immediately in the opposite doorway. A patient, genial smile was on his lips. These days his uncle looked more like a professor than a policeman, Jared thought.

"Cooking is an ongoing process," Andrew informed him as he walked into the room. "There is never a 'last lesson.'"

Rose was right behind her husband. From the slightly ruffled appearance of her clothing, Jared had a sneaking suspicion that maybe his unscheduled appearance had interrupted something. Rose caught his eye and shook her head, as if to tell him not to say anything. Humoring her husband, she gave her nephew a wink. "You keep learning until you're taken off to that big kitchen in the sky."

"Amen to that," Andrew chimed in, giving her a quick kiss on the cheek, an opportunity he'd professed he was never going to take for granted, not even until his dying day.

With a grin, Jared cleared his throat. "Well, I'm not about to be taken off to the big kitchen in the sky, but I am short on time...."

Andrew laughed. "Then I guess we'd better get to it." And they did.

Chapter 2

The nature of Detective Jared Cavanaugh's work did not allow him to clock in and clock out. It demanded his attendance 24/7. When he worked, he worked hard. And because of this, he played even harder when he had the opportunity.

Last night he'd gone to his local police haunt, the one he frequented when he wanted to just be himself, the second son of Brian Cavanaugh. Because he was slipping into character in less than twenty-four hours, he'd spent most of the evening at Malone's in the company of an attractive blonde who had indicated to him several different times that she would have been more than willing to see the night end with him in her bed. He'd been tempted, but he needed a clear head to face the following day. So with much regret, he took a rain check. A rain check he had every intention of using when he had the chance.

He enjoyed living life to the fullest, drinking deeply from the well before continuing on his journey.

The same set of rules that governed his life had him sitting here this morning, for probably the last morning in at least several weeks to come, at his uncle's table. Enjoying being part of the family.

Jared knew from an early age that he was born lucky and he never took that fact for granted. His line of work, amid the dregs of society, only brought it home to him that much more clearly.

He was a Cavanaugh, part of *the* Cavanaughs, and family mattered.

In total, the Cavanaugh family had nine police detectives, one chief of detectives, one retired police chief, an assistant district attorney and a vet. But even the latter was involved with the force. His cousin Patience treated the dogs that were part of the department's K-9 squad. It was that very connection that had led her to meet the man she was eventually to marry. Brady was partnered with a German shepherd and now they were both partnered with Patience.

When they all showed up at breakfast with their various partners and a number of short people who'd been added to the grand total, the custom-made kitchen table needed all of its leaves. It took up most of the room, leaving very little space for Uncle Andrew to operate in.

It didn't matter since Andrew always seemed to manage, no matter how many people showed up for a meal. And somehow, the food just kept on coming out of that vast cornucopia his uncle called a refrigerator. There were times when Jared could have sworn Andrew was part magician. Other times, he was sure of it.

This morning saw only half the Cavanaugh brood. Various appointments and duties kept them away. Jared found himself wishing that he could see them all this morning. It was the same wish he always had just before going under cover. There was something about the danger of the situation that both thrilled him and made him oddly sentimental, making him feel that he needed to see his family one last time before he took on another life.

Not that he was about to admit this to any of his relatives, he thought, helping himself to a huge stack of his uncle's pancakes. He smiled at his Aunt Rose as she passed him the syrup dispenser she'd just refilled.

Undercover work made him hungry.

His eyes swept over the group again, memorizing expressions, absorbing scents and sounds as if they would somehow sustain him until the next time. Then burying them deep inside for future viewing.

This assignment was different from the ones he usually took. The other personas he'd taken on had lived on the fringes of society, associating with the dregs of humanity, a fact that made him doubly grateful to have the family he did. This time, though, he was going to be entering a world filled with a better class of people.

At least on the surface, he amended, digging into his meal. If what the witness said was true, the restaurant was a front for money laundering. The only thing that set the people involved apart from the usual class he dealt with was that the former bunch wore better clothes and had nicer homes.

But dirt was dirt no matter how you dressed it up.

"You seem a little preoccupied."

Jared started as he realized that Andrew was standing at his elbow, a platter in hand. The man had bent over to whisper in his ear. There was concern on his uncle's face. "Sure you got everything down?"

"I'm aces, Uncle 'Drew," Jared said, grinning.

"He's just getting in character," Janelle, his sister commented. She was the only attorney in the lot, other than his cousin Callie's husband, the Honorable Judge Brenton Montgomery. Her eyes were shining as she looked across the table at her big brother. "Don't worry about him, Uncle Andrew. He's in his element. He really likes to playing pretend, don't you, Jared?"

Her playful tone masked the fact that, like the others, she was concerned about Jared. About the way he left himself open, vulnerable to retaliation, without benefit of backup close by.

Concern and fear were things they all had to make peace with in their own way. It was something they all had to live with.

Alex, his cousin Clay's little boy, looked at him with eyes as wide as saucers. "You're playing pretend? Can I play, too?"

Jared laughed, absorbing the noise, the warmth and the good-natured teasing. Hoping it would somehow last inside of him until the next time he could see them.

"Maybe some other time, sport." The disappointment he saw registering on the boy's small face had him adding, "Tell you what, when I get back, we'll play anything you like."

"When will you get back?" Alex pressed, echoing a question that occurred to several of the others at the table.

"I'm not sure, but the second I do, you'll be the first one I look up."

Alex looked thoughtful for a moment, then stuck out his hand. "Deal?"

"Deal," Jared declared, shaking the small hand. He looked over the boy's head toward Clay. "He's just like you were at his age. Except he's a lot more likable." He winked at the boy, who beamed broadly. "Digs right in and wants to pin you down."

"Everybody wants to pin you down," Dax interjected.

Like Troy and Janelle, Dax had made a special effort to be here this morning for their brother. No one knew how long Jared would be gone or when they would see him again. There was no set timetable for the kind of assignments Jared took on. A week, two, a year;

he would have to keep at it until either the job was done or his cover was blown. Jared's father was the only one who was kept fully apprised of everything that went on at the station house.

At that moment Andrew made the short trip from the stove back to the table. In his oven-mittened hand he was holding another helping of his special French toast, something that was always welcomed at breakfast. "You need anything, you call," he instructed Jared.

"Careful, Dad," Teri warned. "Otherwise you're going to get calls in the middle of the night for an emergency food run."

Andrew laughed, obviously enjoying the idea. "Wouldn't mind that, either."

He was only half kidding, Jared thought. Again he was struck by the thought that he was one of the lucky ones who walked this earth. If he wanted a best friend, someone to confide in, or even a child to borrow for the afternoon in order to enjoy the fruits of a familial relationship without having to be tied down by the same, it was all right here, waiting for him.

He felt sorry for anyone who was deprived of these things. Nothing beat having a family as a support group.

It was something that Maren Minnesota could only fantasize about.

She'd never known a large family, never known what it was like to feel a mother's touch. But rather than deprived, she thought of herself much in the same terms that Jared did. She felt lucky. Lucky to have someone like Joe Collins, "Papa Joe", in her life for as long as she could remember. He cared for her. It was because of him that she was here, working at Rainbow's End.

It was because of him that she was *anywhere*, she thought, not for the first time. The tall, broad-shouldered man had taught her how to look on the bright side of life, to see the good in everything and to never be afraid of going after what she wanted.

She owed him so much and she meant to pay on that debt every day of both their lives.

As was her custom, she came into work early and opened the place up. This morning it was the produce man and the butcher whose deliveries she anticipated. She had them all on rotating schedules. Some came every day, others every two days, making their deliveries in the early morning hours so that by the time the doors opened at eleven-thirty, everything was running like proverbial clockwork.

Maren liked being in control, liked being on top of things and prided herself on being able to meet every emergency with some sort of a contingency plan. She'd come here two days after graduation, her business degree still warm, and gone right to work. That was a little more than five years ago, and she hadn't stopped since.

After signing for two deliveries, she entered her office and paused to flip the page on her calendar. She'd just passed the new guy, Jared, as he was coming in to work. He'd surprised her and the word "hello" had all but backed up in her mouth.

Maren realized that she was working her bottom lip and stopped. Usually she forged ahead with confidence and rarely second-guessed herself. But she wasn't altogether certain she'd done the right thing by hiring this new man. She'd hired him on impulse after seeing him in action. Not hiring him would have been on impulse, too, she silently pointed out. Not hiring someone because they were too good-looking wasn't exactly a credible reason.

Just a gut instinct geared strictly toward self-preservation.

She shook her head, laughing at herself. What self-preservation? It wasn't as if they were going to spontaneously combust within five feet of one another. And it wasn't as if she was going to have anything to do with the man outside of the confines of work, she silently insisted. Maren sat down at her desk and picked up the coffee that Max had brought her.

There was nothing to be uneasy about.

Unless, of course, the new man couldn't cook.

Jared couldn't make up his mind whether or not his so-called boss was a genuine ice princess, or if Maren Minnesota just believed that there was a strict dividing line between management and staff.

Or if it was something about him that made her act icy.

The thought nagged at him. Granted he'd only been here a couple of hours, but he'd found that women usually warmed up to him immediately. It didn't matter whether they were young, old, married, single, he had the ability to make them light up like Christmas trees whenever he put his mind to it. Women were also an excellent source of information and he made the most of that, becoming their confidant at lightning speed.

But Maren had ignored every opening he'd left for her so far. Other than the chance encounter this morning, he'd stopped by her office twice, each time on some pretext or other. Each time she'd answered his questions about work crisply, without any embellishments or going off on any tangents. He was dropping breadcrumbs right in front of her and she was oblivious to it all, crushing them beneath her size six shoes.

She didn't take up any of his leads.

Unlike April, the salad girl with the excellent lungs, he mused. He caught her struggling with a large basket of freshly washed celery. Gallantly he took the basket from her and carried it over to the butcher block. Beaming, she thanked him and he lingered at her workstation, handing her stalk after stalk as she prepared them for the salad bar.

Ever flexible, he decided to cultivate April first. There were a number of hostesses and waitresses he could work on before having to turn to Maren. No point in having her linger on his mind.

But she did.

"How long have you been working here?" He watched April work the large knife like a machete and found himself thinking she needed to go slower.

"Six months." She slid the coarsely chopped pieces into an aluminum bowl, then took another stalk and began the process all over again. "My uncle got me the job. He knows Joe."

That would be Joe Collins, the bookkeeper, Jared thought. But there was no way he was technically supposed to know that since the man hadn't been in during the interview yesterday. He looked at her innocently. "Joe?"

"Joe Collins." The sound of her knife hitting the butcher-block table punctuated her every word. Her smile was guileless as she added, "Great guy. Heart as big as the Grand Canyon. Maren's crazy about him. I guess we all are."

The man who had come to the department with his story about money laundering hadn't bothered to fill them in on this detail. Jared displayed just the right amount of interest to keep the woman talking. "He and Maren have a thing going?"

He wasn't prepared for her response. April began to laugh, her knife never missing a beat. "Him and Maren? No way." Her mind paused to think, but her hands kept going. "Although, strictly speaking, I suppose it would be all right." She raised her eyes to his face. "I've seen movies where that kind of thing happens."

She'd lost him. It sounded as if April was talking about something unsavory or tasteless. Was the manager sleeping with the bookkeeper? The DMV photograph they'd pulled up of Joe Collins had been of an older man. Was April talking about May-December romances, or possibly something worse?

"What kind of thing?"

"Hey, you—new guy," Max Anderson, the heavy-set man who occupied the position of head chef as zealously as a despot controls a tiny kingdom, cut into the conversation.

Jared turned to see Max waving him over. His weight and demeanor, not to mention his full black beard, made him look like a Kodiak bear. At the moment Max stood in front of a huge pot that was moments away from boiling over. "I want you to watch and learn."

"Better go." April lowered her voice. "Max has a temper and he thinks he runs the place."

Jared nodded. "Thanks for the tip."

He made a mental note to get back to the conversation that had been interrupted, even though on the surface it didn't seem as if it had anything to do with the real reason he was here. Still, knowing everything he could about the people he was dealing with made him feel as if he was better prepared to handle whatever might come up. Because something always came up. It was the first thing he'd learned on the job.

By the look on Max's face as the other man scrutinized him, Jared figured it was a safe bet that Max didn't care for competition in his kitchen. Or maybe there was another reason he looked annoyed at having someone new on the premises. New people were liabilities. The competitive thing could have been just an angle, so much camouflage. It bore looking into.

In any event, Jared decided to make it a point for the man not to feel threatened by his presence.

"Heard your résumé was pretty impressive." Each word out of Max's mouth was a challenge.

Jared could have sworn he heard the strains of "Anything You Can Do, I Can Do Better" as the other man spoke. He all but expected him to pick up a ladle and draw a line on the concrete floor.

He kept his expression mild. "Where did you hear that?"

The man's nostrils flared, growing wider. Any second now he was going to start pawing the ground. Dislike oozed from the man's every pore. "Maren told me. If you think you're coming in to take over—"

"Just want to put in my time, learn from the best, and go home." Jared offered Max his most genial, innocent smile. The one that could, with a little effort, look as if it bordered on dim-witted.

"Oh." For a moment it appeared that the wind had deserted Max's sails. Unchallenged, Jared had a hunch that Max could be a fairly decent man, if somewhat conceited. "Okay, then." He seemed placated. "Hand me some saffron." Eyes on the boiling pot, Max wiggled his fingers in the general direction of the spice table. A wealth of containers were arranged on it in a system known only to Max.

Thank you, Uncle Andrew, Jared thought as he selected the glass jar that contained what appeared at first glance to be red, long-legged spiders. Though he had always been talented in the kitchen, the names of various spices and sauces, as well as elaborate food preparation had mystified him. But then the assignment had come up and Andrew had taken him under his wing. His eyes were opened. Food became cuisine and he had discovered that there were more spices than he thought possible. Andrew had drilled him until he knew each one by name, description and sight.

Which, Jared saw, now turned out to be extremely fortunate.

Handing the jar to Max, the latter proceeded to undertake a running commentary on what he was doing. Unlike Andrew, Jared thought, Max sounded extremely full of himself.

"You have to hold the slotted spoon just so as you stir the spaghetti or—"

A particularly loud *thwack* resonated behind them, at the table where he had left April chopping celery. Celery, it was apparent, wasn't the only thing that April had chopped.

For the second time in the two days since he'd made her acquaintance, April screamed. Unlike the scream she'd let out yesterday, which had only been filled with surprise and a touch of fear, this one had a blood-curdling quality about it.

"What the hell?" Max exclaimed. The sentence abruptly terminated, to be replaced by, "Oh my God," as

Max looked in April's direction. The next moment, he was clutching his less than strong stomach, a gurgling sound escaping his lips.

"My finger!" April shrieked, staring at the blood as it gushed with horrified eyes. "I cut my finger! Oh my God, my God, I cut my finger off. I—"

Instantly alert, ignoring the gagging sounds behind him, Jared grabbed one of the small white towels that seemed to be placed on every flat surface in the kitchen not directly in the way of a flame. He only glanced at it to make sure it was clean. The bleeding had to be stopped at all costs.

He almost collided with Maren, who had raced out of her office to see what the excitement was this time. "Sorry," he bit off. Even as he said it, he was wrapping the towel around the bleeding digit. Finished, he raised April's hand up high over her head. All the color had drained out of her face.

"Hold it up," he ordered.

But the second he released her hand, it sank down, as if all the bones inside of it had liquefied. "I can't," April wailed. "I…think…I'm…going to…pass…out."

"No, you're not." There was no nonsense in his voice, an order issued to a subordinate.

For a second his command seemed to jolt her to her senses. April attempted to do she was told. But the sight of her own blood, coupled with the trauma of the event and fear had her sinking against him like a bag stuffed with used tissues.

Frustrated, Jared raised April's arm and held it up high, his other arm wrapped around her waist to support her. He looked around for help and saw Maren. He didn't hesitate. "Get some ice and something to put the severed part in. We have to pack it and get her to the hospital right away."

With every word he uttered, April looked as if she was getting weaker and weaker. The next thing he knew, her eyes had rolled to the back of her head and she sank bonelessly against him. He had no choice but to scoop her up into his arms, balancing her so that he could keep her one hand up in the air.

The next thing he was aware of was Maren returning to his side. She held a bag crammed with ice in her hand.

"You're going to have to put her finger in there," he instructed.

Out of the corner of his eye, he saw Max backing away. Jared was fully prepared to have Maren turn squeamish on him, as well, protesting that she couldn't bring herself to touch the severed fingertip. In his experience, most people did not react well to handling body parts, even small ones.

He saw her grow pale.

Maren could feel her stomach rising up to her throat, threatening to spill its contents. It took effort to block out the sensation and not give in to it. She wasn't any good with blood. But this wasn't a time to think about herself. She knew that every second counted. They needed to get April and her finger to the hospital and have them rejoined within the hour if the young woman was to ever regain use of that part.

Taking a breath, Maren picked up the finger from the edge of the butcher block and deposited it into the plastic bag. She tied off the end of the bag tightly.

"I'll drive," she told Jared, nodding toward the rear entrance where she'd left her car parked. "I'm going to need you to carry her into the E.R."

Max deliberately avoided looking at the bag in her hand. "Want me to call 9-1-1?" he offered.

Maren vetoed the idea. "It'll be faster if I just drive her there." She turned toward Jared. "C'mon, let's go."

"Yes, ma'am," he murmured, a little surprised. Somehow, the woman had managed to take the command away from him.

Chapter 3

"That's my car."

Maren pointed her security device at a light blue Toyota coupe. The vehicle squeaked in response as its four doors unlocked simultaneously.

Moving ahead of him, Maren opened the rear passenger door before hurrying around to the driver's side. "Get in."

Jared angled April into her seat before slipping in next to her. The woman had regained consciousness. Hysteria was quick to follow, and she began screaming again. He did his best to calm her.

He took her wrapped hand and held it up while securing her seat belt around her with his free hand. He left his own seat belt open, something he hoped he wouldn't regret as Maren pealed out of her spot and hit the road. Hard.

The woman wove in and out of traffic as if she were in hot pursuit of a fleeing vehicle, flying through lights that had begun to turn red. Jared braced his body as best he could.

"It's going to be all right," he assured April, repeating the phrase over and over again until he'd finally managed to calm her down.

There was a plea in the young woman's eyes that begged him to tell her the truth. Jared knew he had a gift for convincing people of his sincerity in the face of contradiction. He used it on April. She seemed to vacillate between wanting to believe him and being terrified that she was going to remain maimed by her own carelessness.

"But I cut it off," April cried just as he thought she'd finally gotten herself under control. "I saw it just lying there—"

"Maren packed it in ice." He nodded toward the woman in the driver's seat. "They'll reattach it. They can work wonders these days. Six months from now, you won't even remember which finger it was."

A brand new fear entered the girl's brown eyes. They darted from Jared's face to the back of Maren's head. "I didn't sign up for the insurance. I couldn't afford it. They won't— "

"They will," Maren told her firmly.

She took another turn. Because he'd failed to brace himself, Jared hit the back of the front seat. He fumbled for his seat belt clasp, trying to anchor himself before there was another turn. Maren's eyes met his in the rearview mirror.

"Sorry about that," Maren murmured before glancing in the mirror to look back toward April. "The accident happened at work. Everything'll be covered under workman's compensation. Don't worry about the cost."

April's sobs subsided in volume, then finally faded. She hiccuped, wiping away her tears with the back of her good hand. "Are you sure?"

"I'm positive," Maren told her with the kind of authority that would calm the worst of fears.

They'd reached St. Luke's Hospital in record time. After making a left onto the newly renovated compound, Maren pulled into the first available space she saw. The parking lot behind the E.R. entrance was small in comparison to the others, but for once it was relatively empty.

Maren jumped out of the front seat, rounding the hood and hurrying to April's side of the vehicle. The man she'd had misgivings about hiring beat her to it. He already had April's door open and now picked April up as if she weighed nothing. It was cold out and he'd rolled up the sleeves on the shirt he was wearing. She saw his biceps bulge as he turned from the car with the girl in his arms.

Maren led the way into the E.R. room. The electronic doors sprang open the second she stepped in front of them. The area was filled with personnel, none of whom seemed to notice them coming in. Looking around, Maren was just about to grab an older-looking nurse when Jared called, "I need some help here!"

Redirected by the entreaty, the nurse Maren was about to buttonhole terminated her conversation with an orderly and focused on the situation.

"What happened?" the matronly looking woman asked Jared.

He rattled off the particulars of the incident quickly and crisply, ending by saying, "Her fingertip was packed in ice."

The dark-skinned woman whose badge proclaimed her to be Rowena O'Brien looked expectantly from him to Maren. "Where is it?"

"Right there." Jared nodded toward Maren. The latter quickly produced the plastic bag out of her purse.

Pleased, the nurse nodded her approval. "Good work." Scanning the area, she pointed toward the first empty bed that came into view. Long floor-to-ceiling curtains separated each bed from its brethren. "Put her right there," the nurse instructed.

Maren noticed that Jared placed the girl on the gurney as if he were handling something delicate and precious. His compassion impressed her more than the way he conducted himself in an emergency situation.

April clutched at his arm as he began to withdraw.

A fresh wave of panic had entered her eyes. "Are you going?"

Jared paused to squeeze her good hand, communicating support and comfort as best he could. "We'll be right outside," he promised. "In the waiting room."

The nurse indicated outer doors that would take them there. It was only as he followed Maren through them that he realized he was still wearing his apron. He slipped the loop off his neck and took off the apron, bunching it up in his hand like an unwanted appendage. He dropped it in the first empty chair he came to.

They had their choice of places to sit since the waiting room was largely empty.

"I take it you've been here before." Maren took the seat beside him.

She looked restless, he thought, as if she didn't want to be here. Two of his cousins hated hospitals. His uncle Mike had died in one, Aurora General. A bullet to the chest in the line of duty had taken him permanently away from them.

He shrugged in response to her question. "One emergency room is pretty much like another."

A note of interest entered her eyes. "What was the matter?"

He caught himself thinking that her eyes were beautiful. So blue if you stared at them for any length of time, they could make your soul ache. For a second, he lost the thread of the conversation. "What?"

She wanted to distract herself. Papa Joe had been in

a place like this. She was eighteen at the time, about to go off to college, to stand on the brink of new horizons, when he'd been in a car accident. She remembered how terrified she'd been, praying in the small chapel on the premise that he wouldn't die and leave her alone. One moment he was this big, larger-than-life man, the next, she was facing the possibility of his being taken from her. The edifice of her confidence was never the same again because she'd discovered that the foundations were built on sand.

She'd spent the spring nursing him back to health and the summer arguing with him that she wasn't going to college, that she couldn't leave him alone. Eventually he prevailed upon her to go, that he was fine.

Being here brought it all back to her; the fear, the uncertainty. She needed something to get her mind off that. So she turned to the man beside her, hoping for some kind of respite. "Why did you need to go to the emergency room?"

Because my partner was shot buying drugs off a dealer we spent two months setting up. Two cops wandered in, thought we were junkies. Messed up the sting.

It wasn't the kind of explanation he could give her. Jared thought for a moment, digging around in his past for something plausible that he would remember in case she asked about it later. "My sister had appendicitis."

A family threat. Instantly she related to it. "Did you get her there in time?"

It had been his father who'd brought Janelle in, but

he let that part go, nodding instead in response. "The appendix burst on the operating table. Doctor said it was touch and go at the time."

So this wasn't an isolated incident. Maren took new measure of the man beside her. "You're pretty cool under fire, aren't you?"

The smile he offered her was almost shy. Maren felt herself warming to him despite resolutions not to. "Don't see much point in losing your head. Just makes things that much worse."

She liked that. The man didn't fold under pressure. So many people stood back, waiting for someone else to do something, never wanting to be the first. Maybe hiring him was not such a bad thing, after all. "Your sister, how old is she?"

He found it safest and easier to stick as close to the truth as possible. Lies had a way of tripping you up. He'd played so many people since he'd joined the force, the various names were hard to keep straight. If he'd added a different life for each, it would have been impossible. Besides, something told him that Maren Minnesota reacted well to tales of hearth and home. "Younger than me by a couple of years."

"Just the two of you?"

He was right, he thought. There was more than just mild curiosity in her voice. It was as if she was hungry for information. Almost as hungry as he was, but for an entirely different reason. His job was to find out as much as he could about everyone there and to see how they figured into this tale of money laundering that had been brought to the department.

"Four," he corrected. "I've got two more brothers."

Her blue eyes became almost animated. "Younger? Older?"

He thought of Dax and Troy, both were detectives in the Aurora police department, although neither had ever gone under cover. "One of each."

He watched in fascination as a smile literally lit up her face. "Must be nice."

"It has its moments," he allowed. It was no secret that they were close. All the Cavanaughs were now that they had reached adulthood. "But when we were growing up, my mother would have given us away to the first person with stamina who came to the door."

She laughed and he found himself reacting to the sound. It was soft, like wind tiptoeing through rose petals. He pulled himself back. The important thing was that the ice between them had been broken. He couldn't have done this any better than if he'd planned the scenario.

Shifting in his seat, he looked at her. "What about you?"

He could all but see the edge of the curtain as it began to come down again in her eyes. Maren's smile remained, but it became a little more formal. She didn't give her trust easily and he wondered if she had secrets. Was she involved in any part of the money laundering if those allegations turned out to be true?

"What do you mean?" Maren asked as she rose to her feet again.

"Do you have any siblings?" Jared watched as she began to move restlessly around the area.

"No."

There was a note of longing in her voice. Which would explain the wistful look in her eyes when he'd mentioned his siblings. He turned as she drifted toward the TV mounted on the wall in the far corner. "You're an only child, then."

The shrug was casual, dismissive. "As far as I know."

It was an odd thing to say. Unless she was an orphan, he realized suddenly. April had alluded to a relationship between Maren and Joe Collins. He knew the book-keeper was a lot older. Was Maren looking for a father figure?

Rising to his feet, he crossed to her. She looked a little uneasy when he came up behind her. "Sorry, I tend to talk before I think."

Maren relaxed a little. "Nothing to be sorry about. Not everyone comes from a large family." A trace of a fond smile slipped over her full lips. "I have no complaints whatsoever. It wasn't as if I ever really lacked for anything. Papa Joe saw to that."

He cocked his head. Was she talking about the book-keeper or was there someone else who shared the first name? Joe was about as common a name as you could get, other than John. "Papa Joe?"

Her mouth curved more generously. The phrase

about someone lighting up a room occurred to him. "Joe Collins," she clarified, then added, "He's the book-keeper at Rainbow's End."

"He's your father?" There hadn't been any mention of that in any of the notes. He was going to have to get his hands on a more detailed summary of the people at the restaurant.

She crossed her arms in front of her, as if to hold a chill at bay. Instead of looking at him, she'd looked away. "Only father I've ever known."

Which meant that biology didn't have anything to do with it. If it had, she would have said yes and left it at that. He went back to his revised theory and took a shot at it. "You were adopted?"

She was about to say yes, but caught herself. The antiseptic word didn't begin to describe what had actually happened to her all those years ago in that Minneapolis back alley.

"I was found," she corrected. And then she stopped abruptly. Her eyes narrowed like morning glories closing before the approaching dusk. "You always wheedle information out of people this way?"

He grinned, as if she'd discovered his secret. "I like finding things out about people, what makes them tick." He tried to coax a little more out of her. "Helps pass the time. Everyone's got a story to tell."

"Well, mine's over right now." Glancing at her watch, she took in the time. They'd already been here over an hour. Maren took her cell phone from her pocket. "I'd better call and tell Max to be on the lookout for the wine delivery."

A short, dark-haired man wearing nurse's scrubs looked at her reprovingly as he was about to exit the room. "I'm sorry but you can't use that in here." He nodded at her open cell phone. "It interferes with some of the equipment."

Maren sighed as she flipped the cell closed. Dropping it into her purse, she looked around the area. "Is there a pay phone around here?"

"Right outside those doors." The nurse pointed toward the ones leading into the main wing of the hospital. Turning back, the man paused to look at Jared. His eyes narrowed as he studied his face. It was obvious that he was trying to place him. "Excuse me, do I know you?"

Everything inside Jared went on high alert, although he made sure that his anxiety didn't register on his face. Being under cover, he lived daily with the threat of being recognized, being exposed. Of having his cover blown.

The nurse had looked vaguely familiar. And then it hit him. The man had been on duty in the E.R. over at Aurora General the night he'd brought in his partner.

"Sorry." Jared shrugged casually. "But I don't think so."

But the nurse wasn't ready to retract his question just yet. The man looked at him intently. "You sure?"

"Positive. You must be thinking of someone else."

Aware that Maren was listening, Jared kept his response friendly, low-keyed. "I just moved here a few weeks ago."

The nurse reluctantly accepted the disclaimer, but he still glanced at him over his shoulder one last time as he walked away.

Maren's expression was difficult to fathom as he turned back to face her. "He sounded pretty convinced that he knew you."

Jared laughed shortly, relieved that the man had stopped pressing. "I guess I've just got one of those faces people think they've see before."

Maren's eyes slowly washed over him. He could have sworn he felt the path they took. "Just your average Joe, huh?"

"Yeah."

Not hardly, she thought. The average man was passable, not handsome, and Jared Stevens's features were as close to godlike perfection as any she'd ever seen. She searched for a flaw, something that would render him less than perfect, and finally saw one. He had a tiny little scar at the corner of the left side of his mouth.

"Where did you get the scar?"

He didn't know what she was talking about, only that when she moved around the room, he didn't know which part of her was more lyrical, her swaying hips or her body in its entirety. Maybe she was involved with someone with underworld ties and that was what this was all about, he thought.

He found he didn't really like that theory. For a number of reasons. "What?"

"Your scar. This one." She lightly touched the corner of his mouth. Their eyes met and held for a second. Maren felt something shimmy up her spine, dragging a torch as it went. Momentarily self-conscious, she dropped her hand to her side. "Sorry, none of my business. I've got a call to make." She began digging in her purse for change.

"April's parents might want a heads up." Jared handed her a couple of quarters he found in his pocket. "Here."

"Thanks. And April's parents live back east. No sense in calling them until it's over. They can't do anything three thousand miles way." She began to walk toward the double doors. "I'll only be a minute."

"It was a cat." Her hand on the double doors, she was about to push them open when he mentioned the feline. "The scar." He came toward her. "I was on the floor, playing with my mother's cat, baiting it with some yarn. The cat batted at it, caught my lip with her claw."

Maren cringed slightly, as if she could feel the blow. "Ouch."

He laughed at the empathy he saw there. "I believe I said something a little more forceful than that."

She felt bad about asking. "It's hardly noticeable, you know. The scar."

His lips twitched in a smile he didn't bother suppressing. "You noticed."

She paused a moment, debating just how honest to be. She decided there was nothing to risk. "I was looking for imperfections."

His eyebrows pulled together quizzically in confusion. "Why?"

Because she didn't want him perfect. Not if they were going to work together. Perfect was a place for people like Kirk to reside. "It's what makes us all human." The words hung in the air as she went to make her phone call.

"I'm not good at waiting," Maren said when he mutely raised his eyes toward her. Three other people had come and gone, and they were still waiting to hear how April was doing. In the background, a talk show had given way to a soap opera whose dialogue she was attempting to block. "I always have to know things. Now."

They had that in common, Jared mused. What else did they have in common? He dropped the magazine he was pretending to read on the chair beside him. It slipped on his apron and slid to the floor. Jared bent to pick it up and this time, tossed it on the small table where the other magazines were sitting.

"Why don't you go back to the restaurant?" he suggested. "No point in both of us waiting around."

If she drove off, that would leave him stranded. "How will you get back?"

"I'll get a cab."

"Why would you do that? Wait here to find out how she's doing?" Maren was trying to understand, but unless she was missing something, it didn't make any sense to her. "You don't even know her. April's my responsibility."

Despite her innocent appearance, the lady was highly suspicious, he decided. "She looked afraid. I felt bad for her. You've got the restaurant to run. This is just my first day, how indispensable could I be? You, on the other hand, are very indispensable."

It made sense, she supposed. She was surprised he saw things in that light. "Do you always know the right thing to say?"

He shrugged casually, playing a part, although he did pride himself on having a knack of knowing what people wanted to hear. When he was growing up, his father had said more than once that he sincerely hoped his middle son would go into law enforcement. Otherwise, the life of a con artist seemed inevitable for his quick-witted progeny. "I just say what I feel."

"Uh-huh." The man was too good to be true, Maren thought. And she knew all about men like that. If they seemed to be too good to be true, then they weren't good at all.

She had the scars to prove it.

Not like the one on his mouth, where anyone could see. But inside. On her soul. Scars that would never heal no matter how much time passed.

She was about to urge him to leave again when the

inner doors of the emergency room opened. A tall, gray-haired man in green livery entered the waiting room and walked toward them. "Are you the ones who brought April Turner in?"

Jared was on his feet, crossing to the physician. Maren was right behind him. "Yes. How is she?" he asked before Maren had the chance.

"Very lucky." There was sincerity in the doctor's voice, devoid of any melodrama. "I'm Dr. Johnson. I was the one who operated on her. She could have easily lost that finger if you hadn't acted so quickly. We managed to sew it back on. You got her here just in time."

Jared grinned, knowing where to give credit. And how to work the scene. He looked at Maren. "You should see her drive."

The remark had an extremely personal sound to it, Maren realized, as if they'd been friends for a long time instead of two people who hadn't even known each other three days ago. She knew she should take offense at the tone, knew that there were extreme precautions to take against men who looked like Jared Stevens. And yet, at the same time, he sounded so genial that she found it difficult to erect the concrete barriers necessary to sustain her.

Not that she was a pushover in any sense of the word. Kirk had made her afraid to trust anyone, least of all a man who made words like "delicious" pop up in her head. For once the word wasn't to describe anything that he might be able to whip up in the kitchen.

She had a hunch that the only ingredients involved in that sort of whipping were a male and a female.

"I'd like to keep her overnight," the surgeon was saying, "just to be sure no infection sets in." The doctor looked at Jared, as if he was the one to field his questions. "Ms. Turner said she didn't know if that was covered by her policy—"

"It's covered," Maren injected. And even if it wasn't, she thought, arrangements could be made. She and Papa Joe would put their heads together to come up with something. "Can we see her now?"

"She's still sedated. I doubt if she'll wake up for another half hour or so. She was so terrified, it seemed best to give her a general anesthetic rather than use a local," he explained. He looked a little uncomfortable as he added, "If you wouldn't mind stopping at the outpatient registration desk with her insurance information…"

Maren nodded. "No problem."

Jared thanked the doctor then turned toward Maren. They started walking toward the registration desk that Dr. Johnson had pointed out. "I guess it's a lucky thing I didn't talk you into going back to the restaurant." He held the door open for her. "I haven't got a clue when it comes to insurance."

Maren stepped through, nodding her thanks. She sincerely doubted that Jared Stevens was clueless on any subject.

Chapter 4

"I hear the new guy's pretty resourceful."

Maren had barely touched the doorknob before she heard the deep voice. She grinned as she entered the office she shared with her favorite person in the whole world.

As she opened the door Joe Collins turned to face her. It was the accountant's first visit to the office in two days. Things never seemed quite right without him. In his later fifties, Joe still gave the impression of being larger than life. His very presence filled up a room for her, the way it had from the very beginning when he had been her entire world.

She owed him everything.

Maren paused to kiss his cheek before tossing her purse onto her desk and stripping off her jacket. "Nobody told me you were coming in today."

"I sneaked in like the wind," he said, winking.

After hanging up her jacket, she pulled her chair away from the desk and sat down. Slowly she felt the tension leach from her body, the way it always did whenever Papa Joe was around. He made her feel that everything was going to be all right, as long as he was close by.

"The wind, huh?" She raised one amused eyebrow. "Then how did you hear about the new guy?"

"Wind with ears?"

His big, booming laugh wrapped itself around her, just as his arms had all those years ago when he had taken her home from the hospital. From the hospital and into his heart and life. He'd saved her from a system that could have very easily stripped her soul if she'd been placed with the wrong people. Or put her in one foster home after another.

She never tired of hearing the story, even though it had gone through many phases over the years. When she'd first asked the man she always thought of as her father why she didn't have a mother when all the other girls in her kindergarten class had one, he'd told her that she was secretly a princess.

As she listened with wide eyes, he'd gone on to tell her that her mother had been a queen in a distant land. A queen who had saved her from a big, bad ogre, but she'd gotten mortally wounded in doing so. He was the knight who had come by, found her and slain the ogre. Maren remembered always applauding when he came to this part. The dying queen entrusted her infant daughter to him, making the knight pledge to guard her always.

Periodically, as she grew older and brought her questions to him, Papa Joe would revise the story, trimming away the fairy tale and replacing it with a little more of the truth. Then came the time when she'd turned thirteen. After he had swallowed his embarrassment and gone with her to purchase her very first bra, because she'd pressed so hard, he'd told her the complete truth.

Taking a shortcut through a dimly lit alley to his apartment one rainy night, he'd happened across a teenage prostitute named Glory just after she'd given birth. Her pulse was reedy and she'd lost a great deal of blood. He'd known she was dying. Without hesitation, he'd hailed a cab and taken both mother and child to the hospital. He'd left the complaining cabdriver with a huge tip.

But it had been too late for Glory. She'd lost too much blood and had died within the hour. Because there'd been some misunderstanding at the hospital, the attending physician and emergency room nurse had both thought that he was the newborn's father. Something had stopped him from setting the record straight. Alone, with no family of his own, he'd impulsively gone along with the error.

"You wrapped your perfect little hand around my fin-

Marie Ferrarella 59

ger and I was just a goner," he told her time and again. That part of the story never changed.

For three days, he'd come back to see the baby. On the fourth day, she'd been discharged into his care. He'd paid the medical bills out of his own pocket, making arrangements with the cashier to make monthly payments. And then he'd taken his new daughter home with him.

Papa Joe had also paid for her mother's funeral. For three months after that, he'd tried to locate Glory's family. Even hired a private investigator to look into the matter, all to no avail. After three months, he'd stopped holding his breath and finally given up. The baby he'd saved from suffering the same fate as her mother was his.

He'd called her Maren after his mother and given her the last name of "Minnesota" because that was the state they'd been living in when he'd found her. He'd given her her own last name so that she could always feel independent, even though he'd promised to always be there for her if she needed him.

She'd grown up adoring him.

For a second Maren leaned back in her chair, not realizing until this moment just how tired she actually was. But there was no time to kick back. The unexpected run to the E.R. had put her at least three hours behind in her work. There were phone calls to return and orders to place if the restaurant was to keep on running.

She addressed the question Papa Joe had first posed. "The new guy's cool under fire."

Saving the figures he'd just input, he studied his adopted daughter's face as he asked, "Speaking of which, I hear he put out a grease fire yesterday. What was that all about?"

She'd looked into the fire mishap as thoroughly as she could and had drawn a conclusion she didn't intend to repeat to either restaurant owner, Shepherd or Rineholdt. Although it was the former who was most likely to show up. To her knowledge, Rineholdt had never put in an appearance, either here or at the other branch of the restaurant. He was the epitome of a silent partner, which was fine with her. Over the years she'd come to think of the restaurant as hers to run. Hers to make thrive. She thought of it as a living entity.

"That was just Max being careless." He had been the one who'd left the oil standing next to Rachel's elbow.

Joe frowned. Maren had too soft a heart despite the tough-as-nails image she attempted to project. "You're going to have to have a talk with that man."

"Already done," she responded crisply. The man had been warned and had promised to be more careful in the future.

Going into the desktop, she pulled up the software program she needed.

Both she and Joe knew that the head chef hated being taken to task about anything. But the man knew better than to throw a fit or to threaten to leave Rainbow's End.

He was too afraid that he might be called on his threat and subsequently replaced. Maren had made it known that although she was easygoing, she suffered no prima donnas at the restaurant. That was how Max had gotten promoted in the first place. The head chef before him had decided not to show up in protest over a raise he'd felt hadn't adequately reflected his talents. A severance package had been her answer to his attempt at blackmail.

"Okay." Joe nodded. "That explains yesterday, what happened this morning?"

"April got carried away with the chopping knife. Severed her index finger." Maren closed her eyes for a second without realizing it. Just talking about it sent a shiver down her spine.

"Ouch." Joe pretended to shake in response. "She okay?"

Maren nodded. It was accompanied by a half-muffled sigh. "According to the doctor who treated her, we got her to the hospital just in time. He says that she should be good as new. Thanks to 'the new guy.'" She smiled as she used the term. "He took over. Wrapped up April's wound, barked at me to put the finger in a bag packed with ice and we took off."

"Where was Max all this time?"

"Over in a corner, turning white as a sheet and looking as if he was going to throw up his breakfast."

Joe's expression indicated that he would have expected nothing more from the head chef. "Good thing you hired this guy. Looks like he's going to come in handy for more reasons than one."

Papa Joe made it sound as if they were in for a spate of trouble, she thought. "I think we've used up our share of bad luck for a while." She scrolled down the page, looking at last month's inventory. "The worst thing I want to face right now is a head of romaine lettuce that wilted before its time."

Referring to his notebook, Joe input several more numbers, then asked casually, "So what's the new guy's name?"

She looked up. Their desks were butted up against one another, allowing her to look directly into Joe's face. "Jared. Jared Stevens. Why?"

The wide, powerful shoulders rose and fell in a quick shrug. "Just curious. You had a funny look on your face when you talked about him."

She wasn't aware that she had any sort of expression at all when she answered Joe's questions. Maren felt something defensive in her spring forward. "Funny? What do you mean, funny?"

"Softer?" he suggested, not entirely certain himself what was behind Maren's look.

She dismissed the observation. "That's just nerves, winding down, Papa. I really don't care for the sight of blood, especially when it gushes. April passed out and Jared had to carry her to the car."

He closed his notebook and studied her for a second. "Why didn't you just call 9-1-1?"

"Didn't feel like being put on hold and waiting." She frowned slightly. "Why all the questions?"

The smile she saw on his lips was genial. "I just like staying on top of things, honey. With me splitting my time between the two restaurants, I feel like the man on the outside most of the time."

"You? Shepherd and Rineholdt don't make a move without you. You're the most 'inside man' the place has, Papa."

"I can always count on you to flatter me." He laughed, rising. He stepped outside the office, going in the direction of the kitchen. Before Maren could catch her breath, Joe returned. "You didn't tell me he was good-looking," he said.

Maren kept her eyes on the monitor as she scrolled to another page. "Is he? I hadn't noticed."

Joe bent down slightly, as if to peer at her face. "Maren, your nose is growing."

It was an old game they used to play when she was little and had tried to fib her way out of situations. Maren raised her eyes to look up into hazel-green ones that had never been anything but kind in her estimation. "Must be the lighting."

But for once, he didn't smile in response. He looked serious. And worried. "Is this going to be a problem for you?"

Papa Joe must have noted the resemblance between Kirk and Jared, just as she first had. "The lighting? No, I'll just turn it up."

He came to stand by her desk and took her hands in his. His were so much larger, they all but dwarfed hers. "You know what I mean."

Yes, she knew what he meant. Kirk. And the baby who was no longer there. She raised her chin, dismissing the subject before it was even framed. "That was five years ago, Papa. I'm over it."

The look in his eyes told her he knew better. In a way, she supposed he always did. "You never get over losing a child, Maren, you know that. You just learn to cope with it better as time goes on."

She didn't want to talk about it any longer. She wasn't some fragile little doll. Scar tissue had formed, protecting her. She was safe.

"Jared Stevens had good references." She'd already checked on the first and gotten nothing but praise in response. The man she'd spoken to had told her to encourage Jared to come back if he found that California wasn't to his liking. "And even as I was beginning to turn him down—don't give me that look, Papa, I was just going with instincts—he jumped into action to kill the grease fire while Max just stood there, frozen. My instincts had a change of heart. I couldn't very well tell Stevens that I wouldn't take him on on a trial basis. There was no reason not to. And I wasn't about to tell him that he reminded me of someone rotten in my past."

Joe nodded his agreement. "Not every good-looking man is going to turn out to be a bastard."

"I know." And then she flashed him a smile. "Look at you."

"Right," he laughed, "look at me." And then he waved her off. "I've got work to do, stop distracting me."

"Yes, Papa," she murmured dutifully, playing along. She went back to her own work.

Nothing. He'd come up with nothing.

Jared sighed to himself as he quietly made his way to the door at the rear of the kitchen. His footsteps echoed in his head, heightened by the silence around him. Everyone else had gone home, even the cleaning crew. He'd waited around, keeping out of sight, until the silence of emptiness had embraced him.

It had been a full week. A week of suffering through Max's tutelage and ingratiating himself to the food servers, busboys and cooking staff, delicately working everyone for information.

All he'd come up with so far was that it looked as if the salad girl had a crush on him. She'd come back to work two days after the incident and looked at him like an adoring puppy every time their paths crossed. Aside from that, Lynda, one of the waitresses, was a major babe and seemed ready to party with him at a moment's notice. If he weren't on the job, he might easily consider it.

But he was on the job and would be until he either came up with some evidence of money laundering or cleared the establishment of unfounded allegations. One week on the job and he knew everyone by name, knew a little bit about their lives, or a lot, in April's case. Getting people to open up to him was not a problem.

Unless, of course, he was thinking of Maren. She'd reverted back to closemouthed the moment they'd returned to the restaurant from the hospital. He still couldn't figure out why.

Restaurant owner Warren Shepherd had come by on a couple of occasions. He was the visible partner of Shepherd and Rineholdt, and liked to come in around dinnertime to greet guests and take in what was going on. The man, with his dapper, expensive suits and east coast way of talking, reminded him of an aging Mafia chieftain from some old, stereotypical movie. He had a feeling that Shepherd liked playing the part and that perhaps Shepherd's role-playing had set off the man who'd come to them with unsubstantiated stories.

If this was a wild-goose chase, Jared thought, at least it gave him an opportunity to practice his cooking.

"Hey, who put Beef Wellington on the menu?" Shepherd asked on his last visit into the kitchen the other night. He'd stood there, a tiny piece of the freshly baked serving caught between his thumb and forefinger as he'd sampled the dish.

"I did," Maren had informed him, crossing over to the man.

Jared remembered thinking that the man looked as

if he'd much rather be sampling Maren instead of the new dish.

"Since when?" Shepherd had asked.

Maren had nodded toward him as he'd stood off to the side, watching the exchange. "Since Jared made some the other day," she'd replied.

"Jared?"

She'd beckoned for him to come over, then made the necessary introductions.

"This is Jared Stevens, our new assistant chef." She'd come up to him the day before while he'd been experimenting with the dish in the kitchen, not knowing that he was doing it expressly for her benefit. He'd done it to draw her out since all attempts at conversation had failed since that first day.

She'd been so impressed with the serving, she'd asked him to make more and placed it on the menu.

"It's good," Shepherd had subsequently pronounced, one arm wrapped around Maren and hugging her to him. Shepherd's dark eyes had met his. "Keep up the good work, kid." And then the man had looked at Maren again. "Should have known better than to question anything you did." He'd reluctantly released his hold as she'd taken a step back. Shepherd had left shortly thereafter.

The incident had left Jared wondering. Just what was Maren's story? Were she and Shepherd involved? Was she sleeping with him? It didn't seem unlikely.

He found he didn't like that idea very much, although it shouldn't have mattered to him one way or another, except that it might complicate things. Shepherd was the one the department was looking at closely. If the allegations had any truth to them, then the most likely candidate to be responsible for money laundering was one if not both of the two partners.

And anyone they needed to carry it off.

Which might mean the restaurant manager and/or the accountant.

Opening the door that led down to the basement, Jared slipped inside, then carefully closed the door behind him. He found himself not wanting to believe that Joe Collins was involved in the laundering, if that was actually going on. The instant he'd met the man, he'd liked him. Joe Collins was outgoing and friendly. There was something about the man that immediately made every man or woman he encountered feel like a friend.

But then it all could have been an act, Jared thought as his eyes grew accustomed to the dim lighting inside the closed stairwell.

His gut told him no.

He didn't know what his gut told him about Maren Minnesota herself. He was having a hell of a lot of trouble getting a handle on her. The woman who'd been with him at the hospital had displayed both concern and sympathy. She'd even lowered her barriers enough to give him a glimpse into her life.

But once they were back at work, that was all there was between them: work. She was usually there by the time he arrived at the restaurant each morning and she hardly nodded in his direction when he saw her. As for speaking to him, that only happened when he initiated the exchange and then she usually responded in as few words as possible. Icicles filled in the spaces, yet he heard her talking and laughing with the others.

Just what was her story?

Gorgeous or not, Jared couldn't help wondering if he would have been nearly this intrigued by Maren if she'd reacted to him the way most other women did: willing and ready, flirtatious smiles on their lips and open invitations in their eyes. As far back as he could remember, he'd never met a woman who didn't like him and he supposed it bothered him a little that Maren seemed to look right through him. Any opening that had been visible at the hospital had snapped shut.

That was just his pride acting up, he told himself as he made his way down the dimly lit stairs into the basement. He would have to block that out. He had a case to work on, not a woman's behavior to unravel.

Under different circumstances, he would have been more than willing to unravel the clothing the woman wore, he mused.

He came to the landing. This was where the lockers for the staff were located, as well as the storeroom where the nonperishable supplies were kept. He had no idea what he might find down here, but he figured it was worth a look. He had to start somewhere.

Jared paused. Cocking his head, he listened intently.

He thought he was alone in the restaurant. Was there another entrance to the place and had someone come in that way?

He could have sworn he heard voices, or rather, a voice.

Her voice.

Now that he thought of it, he hadn't actually seen her leave. Her office door had been locked and the lights turned off, so he'd just assumed that she had gone home with the rest.

Jared stood listening for a moment, but no other voice was audible.

Walking softly, as if on eggshells that might break at any moment, he made his way to the storeroom area. Max had brought him down here the second day, saying that if he needed something, this was where he'd find it. Maren liked to keep it fully stocked with all the ingredients they used. Shipments came in daily. The excess was stored down here. This was also the area where the auxiliary freezer was kept.

He definitely heard Maren's voice. Jared all but crept the rest of the way until he was within range of the wire-encased area.

Maren was inside the large room, checking off a list she was holding in her hand. Oblivious to his presence, she was chanting something under her breath as she scanned the long printout she held.

"Okay, canned peaches, canned peaches, canned peaches," she repeated as she ran her finger down the list. "Ah, here, canned peaches." Pausing, she leaned a section of the list against a box and wrote in what she said out loud, "Twenty cans."

"Need help?"

Maren caught herself before she gasped. As it was, the sound of his voice, seemingly coming out of nowhere when she thought she was alone, had almost made her jump out of her skin. She whirled around toward the source.

He moved closer, hooking his fingers into the wire mesh that separated her from him. Guilt nibbled at him, although he liked the wide-eyed look on her face. "Sorry, didn't mean to scare you."

Her back was immediately up. "You didn't." Flustered, she tried to compose herself. "I mean—" And then her eyes narrowed. Why was *she* on the defensive? He was the intruder. "What are you doing snooping around down here?"

His grin was swift, taking no prisoners as it swept through her, searing all the way down to her bones. "I wasn't snooping. I forgot something in my locker." He jerked a thumb in the opposite direction.

She couldn't get herself to relax. He'd really frightened her. "And what? You lost your way?"

"No, I heard you talking." He didn't bother trying to hide his amusement, but it wasn't at her expense. "Do you always talk to yourself?"

She raised her chin again. She didn't like being caught unaware this way.

"Sometimes. When I'm alone." Because she felt a little foolish, she redirected the emphasis on the conversation. "I'm doing the inventory."

He nodded toward the list in her hand. "You know, they have computer software that probably does that in half the time."

"I know, but there are times I like the feel of a pen and paper in my hand." The smile on her lips was just a little disparaging. "I guess I just like the hands-on approach."

So did he, Jared thought, but right now, the phrase was taking on a whole different meaning for him.

Chapter 5

It took him a moment to get his thoughts under control. "So, do you want any help?"

She didn't exactly welcome his offer with open arms. She wasn't cold, but the natural warmth he'd seen was in abeyance.

"Don't you have somewhere to be?" The suggestion to get lost was barely veiled.

Jared shook his head slowly, as if giving the matter some thought. This was the only place he was supposed to be, until the case either broke or was disproved.

"Can't think of any place." But he knew better than to push. "I'll go if I make you feel uncomfortable." He began to leave, then turned to look at her. "Although I don't think you should be here alone."

She didn't want him thinking that she reacted to him one way or another, even though having him around made her feel restless. As if she was waiting for something to happen.

"You don't make me feel uncomfortable." She raised her chin. "And I can take care of myself." *Liar. You certainly made a mess of your life by hooking up with Kirk. That's not taking care of yourself.*

He pointed out the obvious. "I caught you by surprise."

"All right, you want to help? Help," she ordered, opening up the gate that led into the storeroom. He walked in. Swaggered in was more like it, Maren thought. The man moved as if he owned the place, not like he was anyone's assistant.

Maren scanned the list she was holding to see what was next. "All right, tell me how many cans of pears we have."

Clicking his heels together, he gave her a two-finger salute, then turned toward the shelves to get an answer for her. All around them, there were rows upon rows of shelves, all stocked with different items.

At first glance, he felt overwhelmed. "Um, Maren?"

She stiffened at the familiarity. "I'd rather you called me Ms. Minnesota."

Standing in front of shelves teemed with umpteen cans, he glanced at her over his shoulder. "It's a mouthful," he told her smoothly. "By the time I get it out, whatever I'm talking about might be over." He turned to face her, his right hand up, its fingers ready to be counted off. "Ms.-Min-ne-so-ta. That's five whole syllables. Mar-en has only two."

She wasn't amused. "I know how many syllables my name has—"

She was irritated, so he diverted her. "What kind of name is Minnesota anyway?"

"A long one, as you've pointed out."

He was doing his best to come across genially. Trying to get on her good side. "Besides that."

Unwilling to get personal, she hedged her answer. "It's Native American."

Jared cocked his head, studying her. The light in the storeroom was typical of a basement area. Dim. Silhouetted against it, she looked even more sensual that usual. Maren Minnesota had the high cheekbones, but nothing else about her suggested that her heritage might have derived from the original inhabitants of the country.

"Are you—"

She stopped him before he could get started again. "No."

Jared raised his eyebrows, waiting to be filled in. "Then…?"

She blew out a breath. Definitely a mistake to let him stay. But if she was busy being annoyed at the intrusive questions, she couldn't think about the other, so in a way, it hadn't been a mistake. Her head ached. Her heart felt ten times worse. "Papa Joe gave it to me because that's where he found me. In Minnesota. Satisfied?"

No, he thought, but he was getting there. Slowly. He made the logical assumption her words dictated. "Then he's not your father?"

"Yes, he is." Her voice was quiet, firm. Immovable. Before he could ask another question, she said simply, "It takes more than biology to make a father." She suppressed an impatient frown. "You know, for someone who just offered to help me with the inventory, you're asking a lot of questions."

He knew when to retreat and when to move forward. He didn't want to scare her away or to make her suspicious. But he was definitely making her uneasy. Was it because she didn't like to open herself up to strangers, or was it because she had something to hide?

For now, he took a step back. Raising his hand like a student, he looked down into her eyes, then decided maybe that was a mistake. She had eyes that entire galleons could get lost in.

"Could I ask just one more?"

Her eyes narrowed. She thought about the old adage about giving an inch and losing a mile. "Such as?"

He turned back toward the shelves, his voice the soul of innocence. "Where do you keep the pears?"

For a moment there was nothing but silence. And then the stillness was broken by the sound of her laughter. She dropped the list on top of the boxes of sugar.

"Maybe I should give you a tour first. Didn't Max go over this with you?"

The main chef concerned himself with making sure his domain remained unchanged. That and putting moves on Kelly, one of the two hostesses. "He just came to the edge of the stairs, pointed down and said, 'The main storeroom's downstairs.'"

She sighed. "That sounds like Max. Okay, this is where we keep the cans of fruit." She pointed out the huge stacks on the shelves, arranged not by size but rather alphabetically. "Here are the vegetables, the additives…"

She continued until she'd shown him everything. The storeroom stretched out for more than half the length of the actual restaurant. He'd had no idea it was that huge.

Maren turned to him once she was finished. "Okay, got that?"

"Got it." There was a sense of order here. If he'd been in charge, everything would have been piled up haphazardly. "Nice system. Your idea?"

She inclined her head, brushing away the compliment. "It's simple." She raised her eyes to his. "I like to keep things simple."

She was putting him on notice, he thought. Jared took a step back from her, silently letting her know that he was giving her space. The air felt rather thick down here, as if it had sunk down. Outside, winter was crisply stirring the surroundings. Down here, each breath felt as if it was just a shade heavy. Right now, he was aware that inhaling and exhaling was harder than it should have been.

"Understood," he told her. He opened a couple of buttons on his shirt, noting that she looked a little wilted herself. "Maybe you should install a fan down here. It's rather hot."

That wasn't always the case. But it did feel hotter now than it should. "The cooling system keeps malfunctioning. You'd think with all the money we're pulling in, Warren could spare some for repairs."

"Warren?" Was she on a first-name basis with the owner because of the time she'd put in, or was there another, far more personal reason? He pulled his thoughts back. That only made a difference if it affected his investigation, he told himself.

Just the tiniest bit flustered, Maren corrected herself. "Mr. Shepherd."

"Maybe you should ask him the next time you see him."

"I already have."

The frown was small, but it was there. If she were involved with the man, wouldn't there have been more loyalty evident on her part? He decided that there would have been. The thought buoyed him. Jared tried not to analyze why.

"It's like pulling teeth," she finally told him.

"Takes money to make money."

"Well, that's a new one," she quipped sarcastically.

He shrugged innocently. "You said you liked things simple, remember?" And right now, the things he kept feeling were far from being classified as simple. "That's something my grandfather used to say."

"Oh, really?" He watched in fascination as a smile quirked at the corners of her mouth.

One of the reasons he did so well under cover was that he could think on his feet and be creative if the moment called for it.

"He liked to think of himself as an entrepreneur-in-waiting." His maternal grandfather had died before he'd been born. His father's father had been a patrolman with thirty years on the force.

For a moment the sadness he'd seen in her eyes abated. "What was he waiting for?" she asked.

"Money."

The laugh was short, terse, but it was there. "You made that up."

"Maybe," he allowed, then got to the heart of his triumph. "Got you to smile."

Yes, he did, she thought, but smiling was not part of what she was supposed to be doing. "I'm not down here to smile, Stevens. I'm down here to do the inventory."

Using the last name he'd given her just made him that much more aware of the deception he was perpetrating. "Think you can call me by my first name instead?"

"So that you can call me Maren?"

"No, because I like the sound of it better, coming from you, but a trade-off might be nice."

It was time they got back to work. Maren picked up the inventory list again and looked at the last thing she'd checked off. "Pears, Stevens. How many?"

With a nod of his head, he turned toward the stacks and began to count.

Because she read and he counted, it went more quickly. Just as he'd predicted. They even did a quick inventory of things that were in the large walk-in refrigerator. He noted that the lock looked defective. She'd responded that she had it on the list of things to fix that she'd given to Shepherd for his okay. It was evident to Jared that she didn't like being placed in the position of having to wait for approval.

Forty minutes later, the entire inventory for the month was done, along with the automatic list of things she needed to restock.

"Thanks for helping." Maren flipped off the light after locking the door to the room. She turned on her heel and walked toward the stairs.

"Don't mention it," he murmured as he followed her up.

With nowhere else to look in the narrow area, Jared was almost forced to watch every step she took. Forced to watch the way her hips swayed just the smallest fraction of an inch either way as she took each step.

The rhythm reeled him in, warming his blood. Triggering things inside him that had nothing to do with investigations or money laundering allegations. He caught himself really wishing that she wasn't one of the people in the case he was working.

Had they met on the outside, she was definitely the kind of woman who would make him look twice. And cause his mouth to water.

Walking out into the kitchen, he waited for her to lock the door to the basement. The woman had put in a fifteen-hour-plus day and he could still catch a whiff of her perfume. His sister had complained that scents faded after an hour or so, no matter how expensive it was. Why couldn't hers fade?

He knew it was important to keep his personal distance. But at times, it was hard to separate the cop from the man.

Grabbing his jacket, he followed her to her office. She put the inventory on her desk. He squashed the desire to take her into his arms and kiss her. Or thought he did. "You going home?"

He was leaning indolently against the doorjamb. Looking too sexy for her own damn good. "It's after eleven," she snapped. "I have to be here by eight. Where else would I go?"

He moved his shoulders in a half shrug. "Oh, I don't know, maybe for a walk on the beach."

She frowned at the suggestion. Only because she found it so romantic. "It's winter."

"The beach is still there." He took a step into the office. His eyes coaxed her even as she tried to resist. "And we'd probably have it all to ourselves."

"Sorry, not in the market for a beach." She looked at him pointedly.

His easygoing smile managed to work its way under her skin even though she was trying to be vigilant. "I'm not thinking of buying it, just walking on it," he countered.

She took her purse out of the drawer and then locked it again, slipping the key into her pocket. "No one's stopping you."

He took a step closer to her. Took away some of the oxygen around her. His eyes seemed to pin her down. "What are you afraid of, Ms. Minnesota?"

She bristled at the implication. That she was afraid of him. He posed no threat. It was her own vulnerability, especially tonight, that was the threat. "I'm not afraid, I'm tired."

He coaxed, just the slightest bit. "More to life than just work. All those stars out, they might just invigorate you."

"I have to get to bed." Realizing the opening she'd given him, she added firmly, "Alone."

Jared inclined his head, a well-meaning employee, playing along. "A short walk, then."

"Don't you ever give up?"

"Not easily," he told her.

She wanted to say no, but there were nights when she didn't like being alone. Nights when she felt so lonely, she ached. Those were the nights she usually went to see Papa Joe. But it was late and she didn't want to bother him. Didn't want to see the concern in his eyes. She hated worrying him.

But she didn't want to go home and fall asleep with the television set on the way she did when things from the past haunted her. The way they did tonight. She felt something welling up in her throat and bit on her lower lip. She wasn't going to think about it. Wasn't going to cry. Especially not in front of Jared. Verbally sparring with him kept her from dwelling on the pain.

Maren took her coat from the rack in the office and began to slip it on. Jared moved behind her and helped her put it on.

Pulling her hair from out of the coat, she turned to face him.

"All right," she relented. "A short one."

"Five steps, ten, more, your choice." He grinned as he held open the front door for her.

Jared waited as she locked up and pressed in the security code. Her back was to him, as if to block out his view of her fingers. He wondered what she'd say if she knew that he already knew the code.

When she turned from the door, he held out his hand for hers. "Ready?"

Pulling the collar up around her, Maren ignored his hand and began to walk around to the rear of the building. Beyond the spacious parking lot in the back, an empty beach stood waiting, separated by only a knee-high distressed brick wall. Jared swung his legs over with ease, then helped her.

The moon was out, bleaching the sands until they appeared almost white. Stars dusted the otherwise black sky. It was a night made for lovers. Too bad he was working, Jared thought.

She grudgingly took his hand and stepped over the wall. He glanced down at her footwear. She wore heels that were at least three inches high, if not more.

"You might want to take those off," he said.

Maren looked reluctant, then gave in. He stood still as she held on to his shoulder with one hand, slipping the shoes off with the other. When he reached to take them from her, she held the shoes to her. He laughed, dropping his hand. Jared began to walk. "I wasn't going to steal them."

She fell into step beside him. The sand was cool against her feet rather than cold the way she'd expected. "I prefer handling my own things."

He slanted a look at her face, then went on looking out into the blurred distance. They were the only two people on the beach. "How long have you been this distrusting? Or is it just me you don't trust?"

"I'm not distrusting." The defensive tone was back in her voice. "I just like carrying my own load."

"Shoes are hardly a load." Moving one step ahead of her, he looked back to peer at her face as they walked. "It is me, isn't it?"

She didn't answer him directly. Instead she stared straight ahead, trying to keep other thoughts from invading her mind. "You remind me of someone."

He knew very little about her. Only the things that could be pulled from school records. Her personal life had managed to exist under any radar he'd had available to him. "And he was a bastard?"

His directness made her laugh despite herself. "Not at first." Memories pushed their way through the cracks. "At first he was wonderful."

"So far, I can see the similarity," he said.

Amusement rose and she was secretly grateful for it. "He wasn't quite as cocky as you, but then, he was younger."

"How much younger?" Pressing his opportunity, he tried to take advantage of the situation and to coax any information he could out of her.

A heaviness pressed itself against her chest as she remembered. "We were in college together."

"And he broke your heart."

"And he broke my heart," she whispered more to herself than to him. Memories began to overpower her, the bad swallowing up the precious good.

How could anyone hurt someone like her? "You're right. He was a bastard."

She wasn't going to cry, she wasn't. Thoughts of Kirk had long since stopped hurting. But thinking of him ushered in thoughts of Melissa, the baby who died from SIDS. Those thoughts, she knew, would never stop hurting.

She shrugged. "He was a man."

He didn't want her thinking that way. Shutting him

out. Then again, he was the one lying to her about his life, and when she found out the truth, he would be dead to her.

Still, he heard himself defending his ilk. "The two are not necessarily equivalent."

"Right." She nodded her head. "I should have said a good-looking man."

He knew that, because he looked the way he did, the amount of effort he had to put forth to get around women was a great deal less than the average man had to expend. He'd never had it work against him before. "That's much too narrow-minded for someone like you."

Maren abruptly stopped walking and looked at him, her temper flaring. She knew she was overreacting, but she couldn't help it. Because today was the day it was, her nerves were all close to the surface. She'd managed to keep them under control all day, but now she was on overload.

"How would you know about someone like me?" she demanded hotly. "You don't know anything about me."

This display of temper caught him off guard. He spoke softly, gently, as if he was trying to disarm an emotional possible suspect. He supposed, in a way, he was.

"I know that you're fair. That you care about the people you work with. That you're not just some boss, pushing people around, interested only in getting ahead and nothing more. I saw the way you were with April...."

He saw tears shimmering in her eyes and felt something tugging on his heart. He hated to see a woman cry. From as far back as he could remember, tears had always affected him. They were guaranteed to bring out his protective nature. Seeing tears in a woman's eyes made him want to right wrongs, to slay dragons, to do whatever it took to make a woman stop crying.

"What did I say, Ms. Minnesota?" he asked softly. "What did I say to make you want to cry?"

Standing here in the moonlight like this, with stars covering the darkness, she laughed at the absurdity of hearing him call her by her surname. She had no idea why it sounded so silly on his lips, but it did.

"Nothing. You didn't say anything. It's just that..." Her voice trailed off as she felt memories squeezing her heart.

"Just that what?" he coaxed.

She took a deep breath before answering. "Today's Melissa's birthday."

"Melissa?"

She nodded, looking away. Afraid that once the tears began, she wouldn't be able to stop them and she didn't want to cry in front of him.

Her eyes stung.

"My daughter," she whispered.

"You have a daughter?" Something else the radar hadn't picked up, he thought.

"Had." The single word scratched against her throat like a cat-o'-nine-tails.

He couldn't leave it alone. She'd put it out there for him to examine and he had a feeling she needed to talk, as hard as it was on her. "What happened to her?"

"She died." Each word she uttered was filled with tears. "She was two months old and I was too tired to check on her." Maren wrapped her arms around herself. The coldness wouldn't leave. "She'd cried all day long, no matter what I did, and then she finally fell asleep. I was so happy to get a few minutes of peace. I remember thinking that she'd just cried herself out, that there was nothing odd about her sleeping so long. That she'd learned how to sleep through the night." Maren blew out a long, shaky breath. Her insides wouldn't stop trembling. "But she wasn't sleeping. She was gone. She… just…died."

Her pain came to him in waves. "Oh, God, Maren, I didn't know. I'm so sorry."

She shook her head, not because of what he said, but because of her own helplessness. "I keep thinking if I had just come into her room sooner, if I hadn't fallen asleep myself—"

He cut through her blame. "You were exhausted."

There was no excuse for what she'd done, or failed to do. Her anger at herself spilled out onto him. "I was her mother! I should have *known* something was wrong!"

"Just because you're a mother doesn't mean you have extraordinary powers. Doctors haven't been able to figure out how to prevent SIDS." Which was what he assumed her baby had died of. "You can't beat yourself up this way. Things happen."

Tears welled up in her eyes, spilling out this time. "This wasn't a 'thing.' This was my baby." Her throat felt as if it was closing up. "My baby…"

Jared put his arms around her. Dropping her shoes, Maren stiffened, resisting. Hitting his chest with fists that suddenly lacked any strength at all.

And then she did what she'd been able to prevent all day. She broke down. And cried. Huge sobs that racked her body. She cried until she was completely empty inside.

And Jared held her the entire time.

Chapter 6

Slowly, with effort, Maren managed to pull herself out of the emotional tailspin she'd fallen into. Raising her head, she gave Jared a rueful smile.

"Sorry."

He'd held her and stroked her head while she'd sobbed. He'd felt something stirring within him, a tightening of his gut, a desire that seemed to invade all parts of him. None of which he could mention to her.

Her cheek was damp with tears, trapping a strand of her hair against it. He moved the strand from her face. "Nothing to be sorry for."

She nodded toward his open jacket. "I got your shirt all wet."

He glanced down at the area. She'd done more than that, he thought. She'd set something off, as well. "It'll dry."

Maren sighed, dragging her hand through her hair. She shouldn't have broken down like that. It wasn't like her. But he'd been so kind....

"I wish you weren't so nice."

Longing threaded through him, weaving in and out like a tapestry needle. "Kicking you didn't seem like the right thing to do at the moment."

She pressed her lips together. Everything seemed to quiver inside of her. It had been so long since she'd leaned, really leaned, on someone. Papa Joe was always there for her, but she didn't want him to worry. But standing on her own two feet made her so weary sometimes.

"I do better when I have a target to rail against." She knew it was wrong, but she shared a confidence with him. "Kindness makes me fall apart."

It was what he'd sensed, what had made him take her into his arms in the first place. What made him want to keep her in his arms now. "You shouldn't let that information fall into the wrong hands."

She looked up at him. The moment and the night seemed to stand still. "Are yours the wrong hands?"

Oh, lady, if you only knew, a voice whispered inside his head.

Jared knew the right thing to do was to walk her back to her car.

He couldn't get himself to move in that direction.

Couldn't even take in a breath because looking at her right now hurt so much. He felt an ache inside of him, an ache that took over and governed his next movements.

Burying his fingers in her hair, he framed her face with his hands and brought his mouth down to hers. Slowly. He watched her eyes as his lips moved closer. Felt the magnetism as they fluttered shut.

It was like a one-two punch right to his solar plexus.

His cousin Callie had teased him that he'd been born attracted to women. And they to him. His father had caught him kissing Louise Rodriguez on the playground. He was ten at the time. Jared couldn't remember a time when he wasn't attracted to women and acting, whenever possible, on that attraction.

But he could also exercise restraint. And when it came to doing his job, he used that attraction as a tool, to help him squeak by if the going got too rough. More than one woman had gotten him out of a tight spot.

But this, this wasn't something he was doing because of the case. He wasn't cultivating the woman, wasn't making a deposit in the bank against a future necessary quick withdrawal. Nor was kissing Maren something he was controlling. His desire, his urge, his response to her tears, was what had taken over, what was now in charge. He could only follow.

He felt as if he were drowning. Drowning in the flavor of her mouth, the scent of her skin, in the taste of the tears she'd shed that had left their imprint along her lips. He tasted salt and sweetness and felt intoxicated far beyond the reality of the situation.

His hands slipped in under her coat, closing around her, pressing her to him. He felt his body absorbing the heat they were both generating.

He found himself wanting her the way he knew he couldn't have her.

Women might at times be his tool, but that was only when survival was involved. He'd never *used* a woman in the full sense of the word. There were lines he wouldn't cross.

Emotions collided with one another as Maren fell deeper into the kiss. She hadn't meant for this to happen, hadn't really even seen it coming until it was upon her. Taking her breath away.

She thought she knew herself by now, inside and out. Felt confident of her next movement. Felt confident that she wouldn't allow herself to be rendered so naked, so vulnerable.

And yet, here she was, naked.

Vulnerable.

Wanting desperately to be held, to be made to forget the huge ache in her heart. She wanted to feel like a woman again. Ever since Melissa had died, she hadn't gone out with a man, much less been with one in the complete sense of the word. She'd become a citadel, a fortress, needing only to work, to meet goals, to make the restaurant the best ever. And to be there for Papa Joe if he should need her. Her life was orderly, precise. As focused as a high-powered lens on a state-of-the-art camera. She felt as if someone had just dropped the camera, loosening the lens and cracking it. Everything was blurry now. Nothing was sharp.

Except for the need.

Her body was pleading for its moment.

His mouth made her head spin, made thoughts fly in and out of her mind haphazardly. Her mind deserted her. All she had left was need. A huge, devastating need. It had been so long since she'd felt like a real woman. So long since the deadness inside of her had retreated enough to allow her to feel.

He'd woken up the sleeping tiger.

She clung to Jared, kissing him as if this was her last moment on earth.

The cry of a seagull, shrill and piercing as it flew along the mellow surf, wedged its way into the hot reality around her.

With supreme effort, she pulled back. Stepped away from him. But her lips felt numb. And bereft. The taste of his lips were embossed on her own. Maren had to concentrate not to slip her tongue along her mouth. Not to give in to the temptation of savoring the flavor there.

She'd already given in to too much temptation tonight. Again, she pressed her lips together. Was she always going to taste him if she did that? She caught herself hoping so before she could bank down the thought. "That wasn't supposed to happen."

"My fault." He saw Maren look up at him sharply. "What?"

"Never knew a man to take the blame for that kind of thing before. By now, most would be pressing to take advantage of the moment," she said.

Was that her story? Had someone taken advantage of her? That would have made her twice as leery. And made his job that much harder. But he'd had a feeling that something was up. "I don't take advantage of women."

He said it so seriously, she almost believed him. Wanted to believe him. But she knew what kind of trouble that could land her in. She couldn't allow herself to start that all over again. Her wounds hadn't healed from the last time. If she got back on that roller coaster, they'd all split open, be raw again, and the process would have to start from scratch. She just wasn't up to it.

Besides, his statements didn't jibe. "You just said kissing me was your fault," she pointed out.

"I don't think a stone statue could have resisted kissing you at that moment." And he could readily attest that he was no stone statue.

"You do know how to spin a line, don't you?" Maren could only shake her head.

Desperately trying to clean his senses, to breathe in air that wasn't laced with her scent, Jared continued to play his part. He lifted a shoulder, let it drop carelessly. "I wouldn't know about that. C'mon." He stooped down and picked up her shoes. "It's late." He placed a hand against the small of her back. "Let's get you home."

She took her shoes away from him and shrugged away from his hand. With renewed determination, she began to walk back to the parking lot and her car.

"I'm perfectly capable of getting home myself," she informed him tersely.

He saw through the act. She was scared. Scared of what he'd stirred up. That was okay because he was scared, too.

"Just a figure of speech." He couldn't do anything about the way she felt over their kiss, but he could do something about the fears she might be harboring about him. "Look, Ms. Minnesota, don't worry. I'm not about to jump your bones." He got over the wall in one giant stride, then held his hand out to her. "What just happened was one human being reaching out to another."

Ignoring his offered hand, she made it over the wall into the parking lot on her own. Despite herself, he'd aroused her curiosity. "Which human being was I, the reacher or the reachee?"

His smile was enigmatic. "That's for you to figure out." And then he paused for a moment. His eyes were serious as he asked, "Am I fired?"

Maren came up to her vehicle. Both older cars, theirs were the only ones left in the lot. She turned to look at him, not certain she'd heard correctly. "What?"

"Am I fired?" Jared repeated.

She did a quick review of his work at the restaurant. He seemed to always be one step ahead of Max, a fact Max wasn't thrilled with but one she found highly commendable. She saw no professional justification for letting him go. "For what?"

"For kissing you." *And for wanting to do it again. Over and over again.*

"You're good in a crisis and you seem to be an excellent chef. Most importantly, I don't have time to interview new people." Still feeling unsettled, she hid behind a convenient excuse. "So, no," she concluded, "you're not fired." She unlocked the driver's side, then slanted a warning look in his direction. "But kiss me again and you might be."

"I'll keep that in mind."

Jared waited until she was in her car, about to turn on the ignition. He leaned over on the driver's side, forcing her to open the window.

Impatience danced in her eyes. She wanted to get away from him. Far away. Until her pulse regained its proper rhythm. "What?"

"You kissed me back, you know."

Maren said nothing. Instead she rolled her window back up and gunned her engine. Tires squealed as she pulled away from the restaurant.

And him.

"I know," she said softly as she drove out of the lot and hit the street.

* * *

It was one dead end after another.

Shepherd had come in today and other than going over a few things with Maren and acting way too friendly in his opinion, nothing had come of the visit. Jared hadn't been able to overhear what they'd been talking about. It could have been next month's menu or a new wad of money being invested in the restaurant. He didn't get the straight of it either way.

As Shepherd took his leave, the man had glanced his way, as if trying to place him from the last visit. Maren had gone back to her office. To input what the man had said? From what he'd been able to ascertain, Maren documented everything.

Jared needed to get a look at her computer. And Joe's, for that matter. Because this getting nowhere was for the birds. His patience was limited.

He'd stopped in at the precinct early this morning before coming into the restaurant. His superior, Abe Glassel, had patiently listened to the non-report. So far, he'd learned that a few of the busboys had had run-ins with the law, but there was nothing serious to go on. None had connections to any organized movement.

The most salient piece of information he'd confirmed, and only through hearsay, was that Warren Shepherd had been boyhood friends with Gaspare Rosetti, who was thought by some to be a lieutenant in the Mafia. But even if this was true, guilt by association was not going to make their case for them.

Evidence would.

He needed to get some hard evidence. Which brought him back to the idea of snooping around after hours. He'd picked up all he could by associating with the employees at Rainbow's End.

It was time to start taking risks.

He'd had that in mind the night he'd stumbled across Maren in the basement, taking inventory. That had been an accident. He hadn't known she was there. He wasn't about to make the same mistake twice.

This time, he made sure that everyone had gone. Timing it just right, Jared had made himself scarce, taking refuge where he could keep an eye on things. Confident that even the cleaning crew had left, he came out of his hiding place only after he'd witnessed Maren leaving the premises.

The security code had been activated, but he had committed it to memory, so leaving after he found what he needed wouldn't be a problem for him. He'd deactivate the system long enough to let himself out, then activate it again.

The restaurant was bathed in shadows. Only a sprinkling of lights were on, casting eerie pools along the walls and floors. He made his way carefully to the back of the building, to the small office beside the lavish one that Shepherd occupied whenever he came here.

What might be difficult, Jared thought as he picked the lock to Maren's office, was gaining access to their computers.

Computers and their software were not second nature to him the way they were to some of his cousins. Mostly he used them only when he was forced to. But the resident computer wizard at the department had walked him through what he needed to know and he was a fast learner. He sincerely hoped it would see him through right now. He just wanted to be in and out.

After sitting down in front of Joe's computer, he pulled on a pair of rubber gloves and switched on the machine. He had no intentions of leaving any prints. He needed to find something but part of him actually hoped he wouldn't.

Not very professional of him, he thought.

Dishonesty had never been an issue with him. But it hummed in his veins now like an annoying insect he couldn't kill. Doing his best to ignore it, he pulled up the main program on Joe's computer. Lights flashed and a message appeared as he tried to open the program.

"Please enter password."

A neat rectangular box pulsated as it awaited the correct combination of numbers and/or letters.

Jared sucked in his breath, then, his fingers poised over the keyboard, gingerly typed in what the tech had told him.

Nothing happened. Erasing the tiny stars that represented what he'd input, the rectangle continued to pulsate expectantly.

Taunting him.

"Well, Harry, maybe you're not as big a computer

wizard as you think you are," Jared muttered. Very carefully, he typed in a second set of letters, falling back on the contingency plan Harry had given him.

This time, the password appeared to take. And then didn't.

"Okay, Harry, Plan B just fell through. Now what?" he said under his breath.

Jared stopped, listening. He could have sworn he'd heard something just beyond the low-grade hum of the noncompliant computer.

Footsteps?

Or was his imagination just working overtime? His nerves always rose closer to the surface whenever he graduated to another level of risk.

Joe's desk, butted up against Maren's, faced away from the corridor. Jared paused in his battle for the computer, wanting to investigate. As he started to get up from the chair, he felt something hard hit his head from behind. He remembered thinking "Game over" as he lost feeling in his legs.

And then everything turned black.

Jared felt cold.

Very cold.

The wind cut right through him, seeping into his bones.

Standing in only shirtsleeves, he looked down to see that he was making snowballs as fast as he could. Every time one was made, he threw it at his siblings who were taunting him. He kept missing no matter how good an aim he took.

Something had to be wrong, he never missed.

And then, suddenly, his siblings were gone, vanishing as if they'd never been here.

Instead he was throwing snowballs at Maren. They were on the beach, just like the other night. She was hip deep in snow, laughing at him.

In front of his eyes, she began to change shape until he sensed she'd turned into something else. Sensed because he couldn't see. She was standing completely draped in shadows.

Jared jerked as a snowball came flying toward him. Jerked so hard that he came to.

An eerie blue light was coming from somewhere just overhead.

He immediately became conscious of the cold. That wasn't just part of his dream, it *was* cold. He was cold. Freezing. Something icy was against his back. It took him a moment to focus. He was in the refrigerator, leaning against a wall. His limbs felt stiff.

Scrambling to his feet, Jared tried to open the door, but it wouldn't budge. He remembered Maren saying something about the lock. It was faulty, that was it. But faulty or not, the lock wouldn't have just closed by itself.

Besides, how did he get in here in the first place?

Events came back to him. Jared felt the bump on his head and winced as pain telegraphed itself all through his system. Someone had to have knocked him out and put him in here.

Which meant that someone was on to him. Or had seen him at the computer and gotten either scared or suspicious. Or both.

But who could have done this to him? Everyone was gone.

Someone had to have come back without his hearing them. Why? Was the computer hooked up to some kind of silent alarm in someone's house or car? If so, whose?

He had no answers and his head was absolutely killing him. Right now, unless whoever had put him here returned, his main problem wasn't who, it was how to get out.

"Okay, now what, genius?" he muttered, looking around.

It was after midnight. Maren came in around eight or so. And who was to say she or anyone else would open the refrigerator before eleven? He couldn't stay here that long, he was freezing as it was. For that matter, he wasn't even sure if there was enough oxygen for him to last until then.

Jared looked around the refrigerator, trying to find something that he could use to pry the door open. If it was faulty, maybe the lock would give. But there were no implements of any kind inside the refrigerator. Only boxes of meat, poultry and fish. He couldn't exactly batter the lock open with a frozen leg of lamb.

Frustrated, trying to think, he shoved his hands deep into his pocket in an effort to warm them. His fingertips came in contact with his keys...and his cell phone.

He pulled out the phone and stared at it in disbelief. Whoever had dragged him in here had been sloppy, he thought. An amateur? But why would an amateur stick him in the refrigerator? Besides, the operation wasn't being run by amateurs. Amateurs would have been caught way before he'd been sent in. He was up against professionals.

Was this a warning to back off? Why back off, why not just do away with him and leave him in some ditch?

He had no answers, only a deep-seated gratitude that whoever had placed him in here hadn't tried to finish the job. Maybe his attacker had panicked. Had he accidentally trod on someone else's territory? Was something else going on here, as well? Right now he couldn't group his thoughts together. He could deliberate on all these questions later. After he got out.

Jared felt as if his limbs would start falling off if he didn't get warm soon. Shaking, he flipped the phone open. The little light on the top told him that his battery was running low. He mentally crossed his fingers that the phone worked and vowed to recharge it every night from now on.

His fingers trembled as he began to hit buttons on the keypad. He depressed 9-1 and then stopped. His first impulse was to call the police, but if he did his cover could be blown. At the very least, if the restaurant was a front for money laundering, Shepherd might have him fired for calling attention to the place.

Okay, he thought, erasing the two numbers with trembling fingers, how was he going to use this to his advantage?

The word advantage instantly brought an image to mind. He started to dial.

It was hopeless.

Maren threw off the covers and sat up. She couldn't sleep. Every time she tried to close her eyes, she saw Jared. Jared, framed by the moonlight, his mouth lowering to hers.

Just the very thought heated her body.

She had to get a grip. She'd been avoiding the man these past two days, but out of sight was not keeping him out of mind. And that was where she was heading, out of her mind.

For two cents...

No, she couldn't very well fire him for kissing her. Restless, she threw herself back down on the bed, praying she would fall asleep from exhaustion.

Any hopes she had were shattered when the phone on the nightstand beside her bed rang. No one she knew would call her at this hour.

If this was a wrong number...

Annoyed, she yanked up the receiver and fairly shouted, "Yes?"

"Maren? It's Jared."

Her whole body responded, going on alert. What the hell was wrong with him? What made him think he could call her at this hour? It wasn't bad enough that he had invaded her brain? Now he wanted to invade her life. "What do you want?"

"Could you come down to the restaurant, please?"

She sat up. Was his voice quavering? "Why?" she asked suspiciously.

"I need you to unlock the walk-in refrigerator."

Of all the odd requests…"Why?" Maren asked again.

"Because I'm locked inside."

This time, she didn't waste any more time asking questions. Instead, she hit the floor moving, heading for her clothes. "I'll be right down."

Chapter 7

When she reached the restaurant, Maren didn't even bother taking off her coat. Making use of only the few lights that were on, she hurried down into the basement and flipped switches as she went. There was something about being in the basement when only half the lights were on that made her feel uneasy.

"Jared, are you in there?" she called as soon as she was near the walk-in refrigerator. She heard something muffled in response, but that could have just been her imagination working overtime.

What if he'd suffocated?

Adrenaline sped through her as she tried the handle. Her effort was met with resistance, and the handle wouldn't budge. Desperate after several attempts, she got one of the large cans of pears from the storage room and banged it against the handle until it finally popped into an upright position. Syrup ran along the handle and door as she swung it open.

The instant there was a space, Jared wedged his way into it, popping out of the refrigerator like a freezing jack-in-the-box and colliding into Maren.

It took her a second to steady herself and to catch her breath. "How in God's name did you get in there?" she demanded.

He had begun to think that he would never get out. It felt like an eternity between the time when he'd called her and when she'd opened the door. Jared couldn't stop trembling. "Getting in wasn't the problem." The words came out in a shaky voice. "It was getting out that was the hard part."

She felt her heart twist inside of her. The man was as pale as a ghost. "Oh, God, what were you doing there in the first place?" The dividing line between them had disappeared the moment she'd gotten his call. Right then, he wasn't an employee or a man who made her leery. He didn't even remind her of Kirk. He was just another human being, in need of help.

Maren looked around for something to wrap around him, but found nothing. She thought of draping her coat around his shoulders, but it was far too small to offer much help. So she began to run her hands up and down his arms, rubbing as hard as she could.

For a second he just stood there, absorbing the warmth she created. Absorbing the warmth her concern created, as well.

She'd asked him something. What was it? Oh, right. What he was doing here? Telling her that someone had locked him in would only drag up a host of problems and questions. He wanted this forgotten as quickly as possible. Only he and whoever had put him in here needed to know the truth.

He decided that lying was his best bet. *And why not? It is what you do,* a small voice in his head taunted.

"I had an idea for a new dish and I was looking to see if we had any duck. I knew you didn't have any in the upstairs refrigerator, but I thought that maybe there was one down here. The door must have slipped after I walked in and I guess the lock sprang into place. It wouldn't budge when I tried to open it."

She shook her head. If he hadn't had his cell phone on him, he would have spent the night in the refrigerator. He wouldn't have frozen to death since they didn't keep the temperature that low, but who knew just how much air was available once the door was shut?

Maren frowned at him, still rubbing his limbs. "You should have told someone where you were going. How long were you in there?"

"Awhile, I guess." He couldn't pretend he wasn't reacting to her any longer. "What are you doing?"

She would have thought that was obvious. Maren rubbed harder. "Trying to stimulate your circulation."

It took a great deal of concentration not to react to her the way any red-blooded man would. Her coat had parted and she was wearing what looked like a thin camisole underneath. She'd obviously not taken much time to get dressed after he'd called her. His blood continued warming.

"I think you've already accomplished that." He managed to curve his lips into a smile.

She got his meaning instantly. But she continued rubbing his arms just in case. He wasn't going to be any good to the restaurant if he had frostbite. "I see you're back to normal."

"Not quite." He looked down at his hands. For a while there, he'd lost feeling in them. Now they ached something fierce. "I'll probably never play the piano again."

"You don't play, do you?"

The grin was fleeting. "Not yet, but I was thinking about taking lessons."

She stopped rubbing his arms. She thought of the other evening, in the storage area when he'd all but given her a heart attack. "Jared, you have to stop sneaking around like this."

The shrug was casual, belonging to a boy who didn't see that he'd done something worthy of blame. "Didn't want to bother anyone. Max always seems to get bent out of shape if I want to try anything new and I didn't want to get Rachel in the middle of it."

Rachel was the woman who created the magic that

they served under the heading of dessert. The woman represented Maren's latest triumph since she'd stolen the pastry chef from another restaurant by promising her twice the salary and twice the vacation. Rachel Bristol couldn't have come aboard fast enough.

"I doubt if Rachel would know a duck from a chicken," Maren commented. Taking his right hand, she rubbed it between hers, then moved on to the other one. She was aware of his watching her. Her throat was beginning to dry. "You said you were in there awhile?"

He looked past her shoulder, trying to think of anything else but her nearness. "I'm not sure just how long."

Something wasn't making sense here. "Why didn't you call me right away?"

The engaging boy was back. "Because I felt like an idiot."

She laughed shortly, rubbing his hands as hard as she could. They were still stone-cold. "Right now, you feel like a Popsicle."

"Well," he began slowly, "there is one way to warm me up." He saw the warning look that came instantly into her eyes and he backed off. Eventually, he wanted to wear her down, but not tonight. "Sorry, couldn't seem to help myself."

"I'm your boss, Jared." She saw humor in his eyes. Humor and something more, something she couldn't put a name to.

"No one's arguing with that."

"I can't just…." Her voice trailed off.

"'Just' can be very pleasant if you give it half a chance."

Suspicion entered her eyes. Kirk had lied to her, time and again. Who was to say that Jared wasn't cut out of the same cloth? That he hadn't done this to get her to rush down here and be alone with him now?

"Did you really get locked in there, or was this just some kind of elaborate scheme to get me to feel sorry for you?"

The grin was as innocent as a two-day-old child. "I'm not that devious."

The hell he wasn't, she thought. She stopped rubbing his hands. They'd warmed up a little, but he still looked cold. "I don't know that for a fact."

Jared crossed his heart, for the first time hating what he was doing. Knowing it was necessary. "What you see is what you get."

She wasn't about to tell him what she saw. A man who could easily bring her to her knees. A man who awakened things inside of her she didn't want awakened. The way she'd driven at top speed to the restaurant just now had shown her that.

He made her feel vulnerable by being in the same room with her. She turned on her heel. "Come upstairs, I'll make you some coffee."

He wasn't about to turn that down. Besides, she'd been avoiding him the past two days. This afforded him an opportunity to talk with her. To create a better atmosphere between them.

To pump her for information, a small voice inside of him whispered. But it was what he'd been sent to do. To gather information from the inside.

"That sounds great," he told her with feeling, falling into place behind her as she led the way upstairs.

She waited with her next question until they were in the kitchen. "Why didn't you call the police?" Dissatisfied with the low level of lights now, she switched on the main one in the kitchen. Maren tossed her coat over the back of a chair and crossed to the urn. "Getting locked in a walk-in refrigerator constitutes an emergency in anyone's book."

Inserting the filter, she turned to look at him over her shoulder. "Most people don't think of their boss when they've done something dumb."

He cut the space between them until he was at her elbow. "I wasn't thinking of you as a boss."

She wished he'd stop standing so close to her. Stop making her feel this itch she couldn't allow herself to scratch. "You have to stop talking like that."

He leaned against the long, sleek counter. "It's after hours. You just came to my rescue. I'm afraid I'm having trouble thinking of you strictly as a no-nonsense boss."

"Well, you should." She tried to sound all business. Funny, usually she had no trouble assuming the persona, especially with a difficult employee. But right now, it wasn't working. "It might be better for both of us if you did." She measured out just enough coffee and water for two cups and within minutes the coffee was brewed. She opened the spigot and let the liquid fill the glass pot. All the while, she kept her back to Jared. The less she looked into his eyes, the better.

"How do you take your coffee?" She moved two cups into position.

"Black." His voice wrapped itself around her even though he didn't move a muscle toward her. "Like velvet."

Black velvet. The words were better suited to the man standing behind her than to the coffee she was pouring. He made her think of black velvet. Dark, luxurious. Sensual to the touch. Her eyes almost fluttered shut.

Maren made a conscious effort to seal away her thoughts. Carrying both cups to the small table on the side, she set them down and took a seat. Jared slid into the chair opposite her. Lifting the cup, he held it between his hands. Warming himself, she thought.

Concern slipped back into the mix. Here she was, thinking about her reaction to him and he might very well need some kind of medical treatment. "Do you want me to take you to the emergency room?"

He shook his head. "No, I'm beginning to thaw out. Nothing broke off while I was down there," he added, holding up one hand and wiggling his fingers for her. A wicked grin on his lips.

Maybe her concern was misdirected. And the longer she remained, the less resistance she was going to possess. Maren began to get up again.

"Well, then, I'll just—"

He placed his hand over hers, stopping her from rising. "But having coffee with you would go a long way to restoring me to my former self."

"If you ask me, you're already restored."

"Please?"

Maren sighed. She knew she should just leave. It was late and there was a full day ahead of her, not the least of which involved finalizing plans for a wedding reception that was going to be held in their upstairs banquet room a week from Saturday.

But she hadn't been able to sleep when he'd called her and something told her she wouldn't get to sleep easily once she went home. She might as well stay here for a few more minutes. Maybe verbally define their respective roles in regard to one another.

Sinking back into the seat she'd never fully vacated, she fixed him with a long look. "You're a very strange man, Jared Stevens."

For some reason the sound of the phony name grated on his nerves. "I know a lot of people who would agree with you."

"Female people?" The question had just popped up on its own.

His eyes were smiling as they met hers. "Some of them."

She didn't get him. Why bother trying to win her over? With his looks, he had to be fighting women off at every turn. What was his angle? Was it just that he was drawn to a challenge? Wanted what he felt he couldn't have? Was she just a game, a prize, a carnival Kewpie doll he meant to knock down off her shelf? It made her feel better to think this way. It helped reinforce the need for her to maintain distance between them.

"You know, a man like you, I'd think you'd have an active social life, yet every time I look, you seem to be here—" she nodded around at the kitchen "—putting in more hours than you're being paid for." In all honesty, he was turning out to be an excellent addition to the staff. If only he didn't make her feel itchy.

For a second his expression was unreadable. "Guess I'm just married to my job." And then his eyes smiled as he watched her. "Kind of like you." He leaned across the corner of the table, his face less than an inch from hers. "A beautiful woman like you should be out there, in the thick of it."

" 'It' doesn't appeal to me," she informed him tersely.

He wondered if she realized how sensual she looked, taking that stance. Things, he decided, would have gone a whole lot better for him if the woman wasn't so damn beautiful.

But he was having a stronger reaction to Maren than he usually had to a beautiful woman. That was the problem. And while playing up to her, he kept getting himself tangled up in his own trap.

"And just what does appeal to you?" he asked.

"Making something of myself. Building a career, a reputation. Making Rainbow's End the best restaurant that I can."

She told him everything she'd believed to be true. Her career had meant everything to her. But in the wee hours of the morning, before the light came to chase away the shadows, something inside her whispered that work wasn't enough.

Something was missing.

And Jared hit the target right on the head when he countered softly, "You can't take that home with you at night."

Her eyes met his. Why was he doing this? Why was he rocking the boat? "By the time I get home at night, I'm too tired to do anything but fall into bed. I don't need anyone else in it."

In his mind's eye, he could see himself falling into bed with her, and his gut tightened in response. "Doesn't sound like much of a life."

He saw temper flare in her eyes as they narrowed. "It suits me."

"Does it?"

"I don't remember agreeing to a round of 'Truth or Dare.'"

The smile on his lips washed over her, unsettling her even as she tried to resist its effect. "No one's daring you, Maren."

She sighed. Distance, she needed distance between them. Real and otherwise. "I guess there's no point in telling you to call me Ms. Minnesota."

"Not after you rescued me. In some cultures, my soul would be forever yours." An almost irresistible smile curved his mouth. "Tell you what, we'll compromise. How does Boss Lady sound?"

She laughed shortly. "Like a horse you'd be betting on in the third race at Santa Anita."

He picked up on the metaphor and extrapolated just a little. "Is it a sure thing?" He knew he wanted it to be. Somehow, somewhere, someday, they were going to be together, he promised himself. He needed it to be true in order to continue.

Her eyes held his for a long moment. "Nothing's a sure thing."

But this was, he promised himself. She just didn't know it yet. "That's all right—" he leaned in closer to her "—I like taking risks."

His mouth was inches from hers.

Her heart had scrambled up into her throat. Any second now, she was going to give in. To him and to herself.

She couldn't allow that to happen. She'd let him kiss her on the beach because she'd been vulnerable. It had been Melissa's birthday and she had been fighting an ache in her soul. But there was no excuse to hide behind tonight. Kissing him tonight would be an admission that she knowingly wanted this. Wanted him.

With effort, she got to her feet, creating space between them. "Well, I don't like taking risks."

The look in his eyes told her he knew better. Jared got up from the table, as well. "Can't grow if you don't risk."

"I take enough risks when I'm at work." She meant

in hiring him, in attempting new things, in expanding the restaurant. There were no personal risks because those hurt too much.

Jared pretended to look around the kitchen. "This is where you work." The implication was clear. He was egging her on to take a real risk, one that involved something beyond the restaurant.

"Jared—" There was a warning note in her voice.

Jared lifted both hands up in surrender. "Backing off," he told her.

For now, he added silently. But he had a feeling that the longer he was here, the harder time he would have backing off.

Though the image definitely did not jibe with the one he normally had of himself, he felt like an iron filing struggling against a giant magnet. But the closer the magnet came, the harder it was to keep from pressing against it.

Once he drained the last of his coffee, he set the cup down again. It was time to get the conversation onto neutral ground before he succeeded in scaring her away. "You really should have that lock fixed."

"Yes. Especially since I broke it getting you out," she said.

Because he was still attempting to entrench himself at Rainbow's End, he made her an offer. "If you like, I can take a look at it."

"You fix locks?" she asked, surprised.

Actually he picked them. He knew how to get into

almost any locked area, provided that the security code wasn't overly elaborate. When it came to tumblers and the like, he'd known his way around those ever since he was fourteen. Reversing the process couldn't be too difficult, he judged.

"Sometimes," he answered.

"Just what exactly does that mean?"

"It means that if it's not overly complicated, I can probably get it in proper working order and you don't have to pay some technician with a logo sewn on his breast pocket an arm and a leg for doing something that in reality takes about half an hour."

He *was* trying to impress her, she decided. Maren fixed him with a look. "If you think you can—"

He was quick to interrupt her. "I always think I can."

She laughed, shaking her head. She couldn't begin to figure him out. One moment he was sweet, the next, he was some Romeo, coming on to her. The only thing that remained constant was that she was attracted to him. And didn't want to be. Didn't want that breath-taking feeling, that rush that always accompanied that attraction. There was always a downside, a payback to worry about. "You're incorrigible, you know that?"

The smile he gave her told her that he knew this already.

Jared picked up both empty cups and took them over to the large sink where the vegetables were rinsed before being pressed into service. He washed out both cups.

"I'll bring tools tomorrow," he promised.

She picked up her purse, ready to leave. If she was lucky, she might be able to get six hours' sleep before she had to come in. "Get your jacket."

He dried his hands on a towel that was hanging beside the drainboard. "I can lock up."

Maren went immediately on alert. "You know the security code?"

"No, I meant I could lock the doors." He offered her a sheepish grin. "Sorry, guess I'm not a hundred percent yet."

That had been a slip, Jared upbraided himself. He *never* made slips. Being around her was definitely undermining his mental faculties. He had to stop thinking of her as a woman and focus on the reason he was here. Easier said than done, he thought, slanting a glance at her. He'd obviously roused her out of bed and she *still* looked better than most women did after half an hour's worth of makeup application.

She watched him uneasily. "You sure you don't want me to take you to the E.R., have you checked out?"

"For what, frostbite?" he teased. "I told you. Nothing fell off. Everything's working. You got here just in time." He turned suddenly and wound up a hairbreadth away from her. "Did I thank you for coming?"

Why did the air in her lungs stop moving when he looked at her like that? Why did she keep gazing at his lips and reliving the moment when time had abruptly stood still on the beach?

She couldn't get involved with an employee, she silently insisted. Couldn't get involved with him even if he wasn't working here. Couldn't get involved with anyone, period. She just didn't want to put up with the hassles, the grief that waited for her at every turn.

"I had to come," she finally said, forcing the words to her lips. "Couldn't very well have my assistant chef turn into an icicle, now could I? Besides, Max would start in again about how overworked he was. I couldn't stand listening to that again."

Humor curved his mouth again as he walked with her to the front door. "So you saved me because of Max."

Her shrug was casual. "Among other things."

He caught her hand. They stopped just short of the front entrance. "You know how I kept myself warm in there while I was waiting for you to come open the door?"

She did her best to sound flippant. "Do I want to know this?"

He didn't rise to the bait. "I thought about you. The way you looked on the beach while you were talking to me."

"I really wish you'd forget about that."

"Too late." He took a step toward her. Feeling things far beyond what he knew he should be feeling. Things that took him far beyond the safety line. "What are you afraid of, Boss Lady?"

Her tongue tried to moisten lips drier than sand. "Smooth-talking employees who don't know when to back off."

His eyes never left hers. *Why this woman?* something whispered inside of him. *Why now?*

"And that would be me?"

"That would be you." She let him open the door and then she slipped out. Standing on the other side of the threshold, she waited for him to cross.

There was no arguing with the look in her eyes.

She'd bought them both a respite. But it was only a small one. And they both knew that, too. The inevitability of what lay ahead loomed on the horizon. Close enough to touch.

Chapter 8

Jared came in the following morning at eight. Max opened the door for him. The corpulent chef, newly divorced, was just finishing up his breakfast and not in the best of moods. Jared went to his workstation and began the careful task of preparing for another day. He got off at six tonight and would check in with Abe Glassel at the precinct at six-thirty. For the time being, until he resolved a few issues, he decided to keep last night's incident to himself.

Though his external, easygoing manner didn't change—he'd offered a smile when confronted with Max's scowl—he was even more vigilant today, his awareness so heightened it felt like the point of a freshly sharpened No. 2 pencil.

After last night's mishap, everyone was under suspicion. Now more than ever he couldn't afford to rule anyone out. Not even Maren. The fact bothered him more than just on a professional level.

Stirring, Jared added just the right amount of chicken stock to the boiling water. He turned the flame down beneath the large pot, allowing the contents to simmer as he continued stirring. At the table beside him was an array of vegetables April had prepared for him to add to the water once it was ready.

Someone had seen him at Joe's computer last night. There was no doubt about that.

The doubt came in as to who it had been and why they hadn't just gotten rid of him. Not that he wasn't grateful, but why leave him alive? Was putting him in the refrigerator to be taken as a warning to back off? They could have just as easily killed him and gotten rid of the body. Or put him into the freezer for that matter. Odds were more than likely that he would have frozen to death before he'd had a chance to come to.

For that matter, why had they left his cell phone on his person? He knew that the assailant had gone through his wallet. One of the credit cards the department had issued in his fake name was out of place. He'd deliberately arranged the cards in a certain order and one card was not where it should have been. It was fair to speculate that whoever had hit him in the back of the head was trying to find out if he was who he said he was.

Were they satisfied that was the case? There hadn't

been anything on his person to link him to the real reason he was here. But then, why put him in the refrigerator at all?

Pausing to taste the soup base, he decided it needed more stock before he added anything else to it. Jared reached for the container and measured out just under half a cup.

Just who the hell was he dealing with? he wondered. Robin Hood?

"You're looking very pensive today, Jared. Planning to spring another surprise on us?"

He looked up from the pot he was stirring to see that Joe Collins stood next to him. The clatter and chatter in the kitchen had masked his steps. An enigmatic smile graced the older man's lips. Was there some kind of hidden meaning behind his words? Or was he just getting too damn paranoid?

"What?

At six-three the accountant was only slightly taller than he was. Their eyes were almost level as they met.

Joe nodded toward the pot. "Something new? Maren tells me that one of your dishes found its way to the menu already. Very enterprising." He inclined his head, his eyes indicating the aproned man at the other stove. "Just make sure that Max doesn't feel threatened. He gets very temperamental when he thinks someone is after his job."

Jared appreciated the opening. He'd exchanged only a handful of words with Joe so far. There really wasn't much reason for an assistant chef to talk to an accountant he hardly knew. But this gave him an opportunity to get a more intimate perspective on the man.

"Is that what happened to the last assistant chef?" Jared asked innocently.

Joe moved out of the way as Jared reached for the bowl of diced carrots. "We're really not sure what happened to Emil. One day, he was here. The next, he was calling in his notice. Said he had a better job." When Jared glanced at him, the older man shook his head. "I don't know about that."

"Why?"

Joe's blue eyes crinkled as he gestured around the area. "What could be better than working here?" Then Joe patted him on the shoulder, his hamlike hand coming down just a tad hard. "Keep up the good work. Maren is very impressed with you. So's Mr. Shepherd." He winked before walking off. "Always a good thing to stay on *his* good side."

"Thanks." Jared deposited the shelled peas, stirring as the tiny bright green globes hit the shimmering liquid. "I'll keep that in mind."

As he watched Joe, the other man crossed the kitchen as if in search of someone. He stopped abruptly when he saw one of the busboys. The older man's expression never changed, but after listening to what Eduardo had to say, Joe beckoned the young man over to the side by the sink. Out of sight.

Turning down the flame still further, Jared quickly

grabbed the two bowls he'd just emptied and moved over to the sink. Instead of depositing the bowls, he began to wash them. Slowly. Straining his ears to hear above the soft steady stream of water.

Joe and Eduardo were several feet away from him. Because their voices were low, he couldn't hear what was being said, but he saw Joe hand the busboy several folded bills. At first, the latter seemed reluctant to accept, but Joe took Eduardo's hand and pressed the money into it.

Just what was it that he was witnessing? Was Joe paying Eduardo off for his silence about something?

He heard the soft sigh behind him. He didn't have to turn around to know that it was Maren. Even if his senses hadn't been sharpened because of last night, everything within him seemed to be completely in tune to her presence.

"He's a soft touch. Always has been."

When he turned toward her, Maren was watching Joe and the busboy, shaking her head. But there was no recrimination in her voice, only pride. She witnessed the busboy hurrying away, gratitude shining on his face even at this distance.

"Papa Joe can't seem to walk away from anyone's tale of woe." Her mouth curved fondly as she spoke about the man who had raised her. "If I didn't stop him, he probably would have given away his house by now."

Leaving the bowls to dry, Jared wiped his hands off on his apron. "He's a rare guy."

"Yes," she said in a tone he couldn't quite read. "He is."

As Joe turned to walk to his office, he glanced toward them and saw Maren.

Their eyes meeting, Maren crossed her arms in front of her. She slowly shook her head. It reminded Jared of his late mother whenever she was about to scold him. Joe cut across the kitchen and gave Maren's cheek a quick kiss. The man, Jared noted, didn't appear to be the slightest bit inhibited.

"Before you start in on your speech," Joe told Maren, "Eduardo didn't come to me. I went to him."

She knew better. "And, what, you just felt like giving away money?"

"Loaning," Joe corrected her. "I'm just loaning Eduardo some money. He's good for it—" lowering his head, he peered at her over the tops of his clear-framed glasses "—unless you decide to fire him."

She sighed. Joe was absolutely incorrigible, and she loved him for it. "I wouldn't do that. Eduardo's a good worker."

"Exactly." His comment was directed toward both of them. "A good worker who's just in a financial jam, that's all."

She fixed Joe with a look. She knew when he was being devious. "And just how did you find out about this financial jam?"

"Carlos told me. He said that Eduardo had fallen behind in his rent because of the usual family problems. Two of his kids got sick and his oldest was outgrowing his clothes almost weekly."

"I see."

"Don't get that look on your face, Maren. A father likes to do things for his kids. Eduardo's good for it. Especially if he gets a raise soon for being such a 'good worker.'"

"I—"

"Hey, Maren, telephone. It's about the wedding reception," one of the hostesses called to her.

"This isn't over," she told Joe, then hurried off to take the call.

Joe turned toward Jared. "She likes to be in charge."

The man's mood was infectious. Jared grinned. "I noticed."

Joe shook his head. "Don't know exactly when the roles reversed. One day she was listening to every word I said, the next, she knew better and started bossing me around. Kids…" His voice trailed off and then he looked at Jared. "You have any?"

"No. I'm not married," Jared tagged on for good measure, in case Maren might have mentioned to the man what had happened on the beach.

"Great invention, kids," Joe said, laughing to himself. "Make you old and keep you young all at the same time. Still haven't figured out how." Maren was coming back to join them. The pride he felt for his adopted daughter was evident in his every word, his every look. "Want some coffee?" he asked her.

She waved her hand at him. "You make ashes, not coffee. I'll get it."

Joe grinned as he gave her a quick, one-handed bear hug. "That's my girl." He kissed the top of her head. "Why don't you come over for dinner tonight? Tucker misses seeing you."

"Okay, it's a date. I'll get that coffee."

"Tucker?" Jared heard himself asking as she walked toward the urns. Both were filled to capacity. The doors were opening soon. Jared tried his best not to sound intrusive, as if the inquiry was natural, without any undue weight.

Was there someone in her life? Was that why she seemed so reticent with him? Or was it just the memory of someone in her past that was responsible for harnessing her when they were together?

When he tried to tell himself it didn't matter, it didn't quite ring true.

"My dog," Joe told him as he followed Jared back to the stove. "Our dog, really. I got Tucker while Maren still lived with me—she's my daughter, you know."

Jared drizzled the finely chopped celery into the pot, then put in just enough mushrooms for flavor. "Yes, I know. She told me."

Glancing toward Joe, he saw that the man watched at him with interest. As a possible match for Maren? It didn't seem likely. Then what? Was Joe feeling him out for some reason? Jared knew that for money laundering to be successful in this set of circumstances, the accountant would have to be in on it. But if he had ever met anyone who was less likely to have criminal leanings, it was Joe Collins.

For the first time in his life, the nature of his work really bothered Jared. The other assignments he'd worked on had taken him deep into the nether regions of a world populated with dealers and drug addicts and arms runners. The very dregs of society lived there.

Occasionally he had encountered people whose souls were not entirely black, who might be redeemable under the right set of circumstances, and he'd felt pity for them. In one instance he'd even set the wheels in motion to get a commuted sentence for a kid as long as the minor followed the strict rules set down in probation. But he'd never had doubts about what he was doing. Never had doubts about the lies he was telling, the people he was lying to.

Until now.

This was different.

These were people he could find himself liking. Under different circumstances...

About to leave, Joe stopped abruptly. "Hey, I've got an idea. You busy tonight?"

Jared thought of the meeting with his superior. That could be postponed if he was on to something. "No."

"Why don't you come over and cook for us?" Joe suggested with feeling. "Show us what you've got? Maren's not much for cooking for herself and me, I live on TV dinners when I'm not grabbing something at one of the restaurants. The food's great, but nothing beats the atmosphere of a home-cooked meal." Joe warmed to his idea. "How about it, you game?"

He wanted the invitation, but he didn't want to seem overly eager and to set off any alarms. For all he knew, Joe might be trying to feel him out, as well. "Won't that be kind of the same thing? If I cook?"

Joe grinned broadly. "Just think of us as your guinea pigs."

"Okay. What time?"

"I knock off by five. I can get Maren to do the same. This is your early night, isn't it?"

As an accountant, Joe might know that, Jared thought. And then, he might have gone out of his way to find out. Jared's suspicions went up another notch.

"Yes."

"Excellent." Joe looked exceedingly pleased. "Come by as soon as you're done here. Anything special you want me to pick up?"

Jared thought of the excuse he'd given Maren why he'd been in the refrigerator when he'd gotten locked in. He might as well play that line out. "No, I've got it covered. You like duck?"

Amusement curved the older man's mouth. "I like Donald and Daffy. Can't say I've eaten it, though." He thought a second. "Duck, huh?"

He was going to make duck à l'orange. Uncle Andrew had walked him through it once. He'd looked it up last night after he'd gotten home just in case Maren thought to ask him any questions about it today.

"Duck à l'orange," he told him. "There's an Asian market not far from where I live and I can get the rest of what I need here." He indicated the spice table teeming with various ingredients.

"Make sure Maren knows. You wouldn't want her to think you were pilfering the ingredients from the storeroom." Jared couldn't tell if Joe was serious or pulling his leg. "Maren's a very generous soul, but she hates stealing. Always be up front with her."

The warning rang in Jared's head, underscoring his guilt.

"Up front with who?" Maren asked, rejoining them. "Here's your coffee, Papa Joe."

Joe paused to inhale deeply before answering her. "You, my dear. You." He took a long sip and looked like a man who had just been revitalized. "I was just telling Jared here how much you value honesty." He looked at Maren over the rim of his cup as he took another long sip. "By the way, he'll be joining us tonight."

Maren was stunned. She was trying to cover it, Jared thought, but she'd had an unguarded moment and he'd seen it. She wasn't happy about Joe's invitation. "Papa Joe, I really don't—"

Joe cut her off, as if he knew what she was about to say. "Maren, the man needs to practice his art. Who better to practice it on than the woman who can further his career?" He paused for yet another sip, then said, "See you in the office.

She turned to Jared as Joe walked away, her hands on her hips. "You're cooking?"

The woman did not seem happy about the turn of

events, he thought. "Looks like." Much as he wanted the opportunity to get in closer to both Joe and Maren, he knew he had to at least sound as if he was willing not to come.

And as long as he phrased it right, she wouldn't let him cancel, he thought.

He added pepper to the soup, his voice was casual with just a hint of disappointment. "Listen, if it makes you uncomfortable having me at dinner, I'll just tell Joe I can't make it."

She stiffened, just as he figured she would. "No, I won't be uncomfortable." Her tone was both defensive and accusing. "Why should I be?"

Adding garlic, he gave her an innocent look, then backtracked. "Well, I thought…never mind."

Maren cut him off, not wanting the conversation to go any further down the path he was obviously on. If she was uncomfortable in his presence, he'd think that she'd felt something and that was the last thing she wanted him to believe.

"Papa Joe seems to have taken a liking to you for some reason and dinner is at his place, so he gets to say who he invites."

A commotion in the front of the restaurant terminated any further discussion on the topic. A loud, booming voice was hailing and greeting people as it came closer.

The next moment, Warren Shepherd swept into the kitchen.

At approximately five feet, ten inches, the dapper, gray-haired man cultivated an old-world courtliness in his appearance. It was mingled with the aura of someone who had once grown up on the mean streets of New York City and was now intimately street savvy.

Warren Shepherd was a product of another era. Even when he smiled, there was a deadliness that was hard to mask. He'd spent years perfecting that exact look. People were always quick to give in to him. He wouldn't have it any other way.

Calling out to April and nodding at Max, Shepherd made his way over to Maren.

"Moxie! How's my favorite manager?" he asked, giving her a hug that to Jared seemed warmer than the situation warranted.

Why did he call her Moxie? Jared wondered. Was it some term of affection? Any thoughts that something intimate went on between the two vanished. Jared could see that Maren forced a smile to her lips.

"Just fine, Mr. Shepherd."

"Mr. Shepherd." Shepherd laughed, shaking his head.

"I can remember a time when you called me Uncle Warren." Releasing her, he glanced at Jared. Recognition entered his eyes and the thousand-watt smile followed. "Jared, right?"

"Right." He decided he didn't like the man on principle.

Shepherd nodded toward Maren. "I've known this girl since she came up to here—" he brought his hand up to his waist "—and wore Band-Aids on her knees. A real daredevil, this one. Used to come here after school and do her homework in Joe's office." He stood back, as if appraising her. Or showing her off, Jared thought. Did Shepherd think of Maren as his possession? "Who knew she'd turn out to be such a looker? And steal half the office away from her old man?" The questions were all rhetorical. It was clear Shepherd wasn't looking to start any kind of a dialogue with him. The man scanned the room. "Speaking of which, did Joe get in yet?"

"Papa Joe is in his office." She waited a moment. When the owner made no comment on the information because he was too busy looking her up and down as if she were a piece of merchandise, she asked, "Do you want me to go get him?"

"Nah, don't bother." He waved a hand at her offer. "The mountain'll go to him." But as she dutifully fell into place beside him, Shepherd shook his head. "Do me a favor, Moxie, stay out here and crack the whip a little. I want some time alone with your old man."

Maren stepped back. Jared could see she wasn't pleased about it, but she hid it well enough beneath a guise of respectfulness. He couldn't help wondering what she was thinking.

"Of course." Maren inclined her head, deferring to Shepherd.

Jared waited a beat until the other man had left to see Joe. "You don't like him, do you?"

Maren continued to watch Shepherd leave. "He's the owner."

Jared stirred the soup, then took a container of garlic powder and added it to the liquid. "That doesn't answer my question."

She allowed herself a small sigh. No, she didn't like Shepherd, hadn't liked him since he'd first put moves on her when she was fifteen. But she needed this job. Loved this job, so she put up with it, making sure that Shepherd knew without her saying it that angels had a better chance of redecorating hell with snow than Shepherd had of ever getting close to her.

"He can be a little abrasive," she allowed. "And he does a really, really bad Robert De Niro impression."

Jared stopped stirring and stared at her. "Come again?"

"Robert De Niro." She finally turned toward him. "In *Casino*." She could tell by Jared's puzzled expression that he needed a little background. And she had time to kill since she wasn't welcome in her office at the moment.

"Warren Shepherd grew up in a neighborhood where everyone either joined the police force or became a 'wise guy' as the euphemism goes these days. He didn't have the stomach for the former and his connections weren't strong enough for the latter. So he playacts the part. Sees himself as a cross between Brando in the *Godfather* and Robert De Niro in *Casino* and *Goodfellas*, with maybe a little Cagney probably thrown in.

Cocky," she added, then shrugged. "It's harmless enough until it turns nasty."

"Nasty?" He coaxed her to elaborate, wondering if this was the thing that would break the dam he'd been facing so far.

"I once saw him really light into a server for spilling a single drop of wine on the tablecloth. He was sitting at the table at the time with his latest 'lady.'" She said the word as if it left a bad taste in her mouth. He knew for a fact that Shepherd was married with three kids. "I thought he was going to vivisect the poor guy right then and there."

Jared read between the lines. "And that's when you stepped in."

She shrugged. "I tried to deflect Shepherd's wrath. It was uncalled for."

"Is that why he calls you Moxie?"

"I guess." She sighed, then looked at him as if suddenly becoming aware of him for the first time. "Why am I always telling you these things?" She was friendly, but she never ran off at the mouth. What was it about him that made her want to talk?

"People say I'm easy to talk to."

His smile wound its way under her skin again. She was going to have to watch that. She'd already said too much, let herself relax around him too much. She was going to have to be careful.

Maren squared her shoulders. "Well, they're not paying either one of us to talk. Why don't you get back to what you were doing?" She allowed herself one deep whiff. "It smells delicious."

"Want a sample?"

That was just the problem. She wanted a sample. But it had nothing to do with what presently simmered on the range and everything to do with what simmered between them. And that, she knew she shouldn't sample. "Not right now."

With that, she walked out into the front of the restaurant and waited until she was allowed to go into her office again.

Chapter 9

Joe stuck his head into the kitchen just before he left and addressed Jared. "Wonder if you could do me a favor?"

In the middle of ladling out several bowls of the soup he'd prepared, Jared paused. "Sure. What is it?"

Joe grinned. "Never agree to something until you know what it is," he warned, then made his request. "Could you pick up Maren on your way over? She only lives a mile away from my place. Here's her address."

"No hardship there." This was going to throw his timing off, but he could still manage it, Jared thought as he pocket the piece of paper. "Maren's okay with my picking her up?"

"She will be." Joe was already walking toward the back exit.

Alarms went off. "Hey, what does that mean? Does she even know I'm coming by?"

"I'll leave her a message on her answering machine. She'll get it when she gets home." He paused a moment before disappearing around the corner. "She's on your way. Why put added pollution into the air, right?"

"Right," Jared said, more under his breath than for anyone else to hear. He hurried back to what he was doing.

Was Joe playing matchmaker or was there something else on the man's agenda? He couldn't meet with his superior this evening, but he needed to check in with Glassel to see if the man had come up with anything on either Joe or Maren.

And after that, he had to swing by his uncle's house.

At six-thirty, Jared followed his uncle into the man's state-of-the-art kitchen. His mouth began to water even before he crossed the threshold. The aroma was pure heaven.

"Really appreciate this, Uncle Andrew."

"Hey, my pleasure." After receiving Jared's call, he'd spent the better part of the afternoon in the kitchen, adding some of his own touches to a time-honored recipe. Everything now stood packed and ready to go. "I haven't made duck à l'orange in a long time. What's the occasion, or shouldn't I ask?"

Jared couched his answer in the vague terms the job required of him. "I've been invited to a suspect's house and asked to cook. Since it had to be something special and I've only made this once before, I thought it might go better if you did the honors instead of me."

"How are you going to explain making the duck in half an hour?"

"I told them I went home at lunch to start the process."

Andrew nodded, obviously satisfied with whatever his nephew felt he could share. He began placing the foil-sealed dishes into one of the two large double-bagged grocery bags he'd prepared. Jared began packing the other.

"Not that I mind doing this—hell, I'll use any excuse to putter around in the kitchen—but you could have done this yourself, you know." Andrew laughed. "Out of all the Cavanaughs, you're the only one who seems to have the talent."

A little of the sauce leaked. Jared licked his fingers, then grabbed a sponge to tidy up the counter. "Maybe we'll open up that catering restaurant you talked about when I retire."

"Famous last words. Actually," he said as he secured the last container, "cooking for this brood keeps me plenty busy. And there's another one on the way."

Jared paused and looked at his uncle. "Spouse or baby?" In the last couple of years, his cousins had been coupling up as if they'd received an edict from Noah to pair off before the flood came. What did come was a flood of marriages, followed by an ocean of babies.

"Baby. Rayne's going to be a mother," he confided, then grinned broadly, echoing the mantra of every harried parent. "I just hope I live long enough to see her find out what it means to have a rebellious kid on her hands."

Jared knew Rayne had been the last word in rebel during her teen years. They'd all worried about her. For nothing, it now seemed, but her antics were still very vividly imprinted in all their minds. Through it all, Andrew had remained as evenhanded with her as he had with his other four.

"Tell her congratulations for me and that I can't wait to see her with an extra twenty-five pounds on her body."

Taking a shopping bag, Andrew led the way out of the house and to Jared's car. "Tell her yourself. I don't have a death wish."

Jared placed the shopping bag he was carrying on the floor behind the passenger seat, then took the one his uncle had, securing it beside the first. He was running late and hurried to the driver's side.

"Thanks," he said over his shoulder as he got into the car. "I owe you one."

"You owe me more than that, boy, but who's counting?" Andrew laughed, stepping back just before Jared backed out of the driveway and sped away.

He got to Maren's ground-floor garden apartment in ten minutes flat, catching all the lights. A couple of times he'd just barely squeaked through. The meal had stayed intact through it all.

She came to the door before he had a chance to drop his hand from the doorbell. "If I'd had your cell phone number, I would have told you not to bother coming by."

"Why?"

"Because I was perfectly capable of driving myself. I don't know what Papa Joe was thinking."

Actually she did. And that was just the problem. Papa Joe was acting on his feeling that she needed to get out. That the longer she didn't socialize with the opposite sex, the harder it would be for her to get back into the swing of things. He refused to accept the fact that the "swing" no longer had an allure for her.

"Well, since I'm here, you might as well come with me. Is Joe big on conservation?"

She followed him to guest parking, where he'd left his vehicle. "Why?"

"Because he said something about it making sense to have just one car rather than two polluting the air."

"I guess when you don't lie for a living, you're hard-pressed to come up with one as an excuse," Maren commented.

Was that for his benefit? Damn, he was starting to really hate having to examine everything twice. He missed having the luxury of being able to take something at face value. But then, he told himself, that was what tonight was about. A further investigation into Joe's and Maren's lives, to hopefully clear them of any connections.

People let things slip when they were relaxed, and neither of them struck him as hardened criminals. Worse
case scenario, they were average people in over their
heads.

No, he amended, the word "average" was never
going to be used to describe anything about Maren.

He unlocked his doors, opening the passenger side
for her before rounding the rear to get in on his side.

The second she got into the car, her senses were sur-
rounded by the aroma wafting from the packages in the
back seat. Buckling her seat belt, she looked at Jared.
"My God, what is that wonderful smell?"

Already strapped in, he turned on the ignition as he
grinned. "If I said it was me…?"

She twisted around in her seat and saw the packages
in the back as he pulled out of the lot. "Then I'd say that
you were good enough to devour."

"Sounds promising."

She tried not to notice the way his eyes twinkled.
"Really, what is that aroma?"

"Air freshener," he teased.

Her eyes narrowed as she straightened in her seat.
"One more time." Her voice held a hint of warning, and
Jared caught himself wondering what she was like when
she lost her temper. He had a feeling that he'd find the
situation more than a little appealing.

"It's duck à l'orange. Once I knew that I was in
charge of dinner, I went home during my free time to
get it started."

It was on the tip of her tongue to apologize for the command performance, but what he said aroused her curiosity. "You have duck just sitting in your refrigerator." Skepticism filled her voice.

He knew before he began that this was going to get involved. But he was ready for it. "Let's just say I have connections. A neighbor who works at an Asian market owes me a favor. He brought the duck by the apartment for me."

"And broke in to put the duck in your refrigerator so you could prepare it when you got in."

He was ready for that one, too. "We have each other's keys." Jared signaled for a left turn. "Are you always this suspicious?"

There was a time when she wasn't, she thought sadly. But that felt like a million years ago now. "Fall-out from a bad relationship."

"Does that mean we're in a relationship? Or about to be in one?" he amended.

She knew it was a mistake getting into the car with him. "How about you don't ask any more questions, just drive?"

The silence lasted all of a minute and a half. While a soft love song played on the oldies station, he said, "You look nice tonight."

She wasn't about to say that she had gone the extra mile, examining her makeup to make sure everything was just perfect. That there had been butterflies in her stomach when she'd heard Papa Joe on her answering machine, telling her that Jared was stopping by to pick her up before dinner.

She pointed to the road. "I said, just drive."

"I didn't put it in the form of a question," he said.

Defeated, Maren could only laugh and shake her head. "I guess no one's ever called you the strong, silent type, have they?"

"I come from a large family. You keep quiet, nobody notices you." Slanting a glance to see her reaction, he saw that same wistful smile slip over her lips.

She cleared her throat, rousing herself. "And you like being noticed."

"Depends on who's noticing."

His voice was almost seductive and made her squirm inside. "I can't imagine someone not noticing you."

"Funny," he said softly, allowing himself a long look at her as they waited at the light. "I was thinking the same thing about you."

Maren was on her guard instantly. It was what had allowed her to survive all these many months, kept her from becoming involved with anyone. Kept her from being hurt. "Why?"

"Because I was wondering why someone hadn't taken you off the market yet."

"Someone did," she informed him tersely. "Me." She pointed toward the curb that ran parallel to a row of condominiums. Joe's place, a single-family home, was close by. "You can park over there."

Joe was waiting for them.

The moment Jared parked the car, the accountant was opening his door to them. The man hurried over to the electric-blue Mustang, opening first Maren's door, then reaching in to help with the shopping bags Jared had brought.

"Smells wonderful," Joe declared, taking a deep whiff.

"Yeah, it does, doesn't it?" Jared agreed, but he was looking at Maren as he said it.

"I'll go in and set the table." Maren flushed, backing away.

"Already done," Joe said. "But you can go inside and play with Tucker. I can't get him to do anything." Jared slammed the door shut and they began to head toward Joe's home. "All he does is sit on the sofa by the window and look out, waiting for you to come up the walk."

"God, but you are good at shoveling out guilt," Maren said over her shoulder as she hurried into the home where she'd grown up.

"It's a gift," Joe confided to Jared and winked.

A little more than two hours later, Joe pushed his chair away from the dining room table.

"That has to be by far one of the best meals I've ever had," Joe informed him as he patted his swollen stomach affectionately. "Only way I would be able to get in another bite is if I put it in my pocket." He looked at Maren. "You know, if I were Max, I'd be worried about my job."

Jared dismissed the compliment with a wave of his hand. "There's no reason for that. I'm content being an assistant for now."

Joe leaned back in his chair, studying Jared. "You don't strike me as someone who's willing just to sit back."

"Not sit back, learn," Jared corrected. He couldn't seem to help himself from glancing at Maren. Every time he focused on Joe, something dragged his attention—not to mention his eyes—away. The woman was the embodiment of the word "exquisite."

"You jump into something too early and things might turn sour on you. Slow and steady is the better way to go."

It was obviously the right answer as Joe broke out in a wreath of smiles. "I like this guy, Maren."

"I think we've already figured that out, Papa." Getting to her feet, Maren began stacking dishes together. The moment she started to get up, Jared rose to his feet quickly. "No, that's okay. Division of labor. You cooked—" she waved him back into his chair "—I'll clean up. You talk to Papa," she prompted.

"One in a million, that girl," Joe commented as she walked out of the room.

She wasn't out of earshot yet. "And don't you forget it," Maren said over her shoulder.

As he'd been doing all evening, Tucker followed her into the kitchen. The dog had spent the entire duration of the meal sitting patiently at her elbow, waiting for either an affectionate pat or a scrap of meat, whichever came his way. He accepted both with equal gusto.

Joe picked up the half-empty bottle of Chablis that Maren had brought with her. "Wine?" Joe tilted the half-empty bottle over his glass.

"Thanks, but no more for me. One's my limit if I'm driving." Jared placed his hand over the mouth of his glass.

"Smart boy."

Joe poured less than half a glass for himself and an equal amount of light pink liquid into Maren's glass before retiring the bottle. "Don't often meet young men your age with a good head on their shoulders." He laughed to himself as he took a sip. "At your age, I had no direction, no purpose. Took walking down a dark alley one night to give me that." He smiled, seeing the slight confusion in Jared's eyes.

"That's how I found Maren. She was about five minutes old when we met." The accountant's voice took on a distant quality, as if he was traveling back over the years to that night. "Her mother had just given birth beside a Dumpster. I think she was going to leave Maren there, except that she was losing too much blood to even stand up. I got them both to the hospital." For the first time, Jared saw the man's expression grow grim. "But Maren's mother didn't make it."

The leap from Good Samaritan to father was a broad one. "How did you—"

Joe second-guessed him. "The nurse and E.R. doctor thought I was the baby's father. I started to set them straight, but something stopped me. I didn't have any family of my own. My father took off when I was born, my mother died while I was in high school. I spent the last two years of that in foster care. Not the best of conditions. Looking down into that tiny face, I realized that I wanted to belong to someone and wanted to have someone belong to me. And I *didn't* want her going into the foster care system. So I let them think I was her father."

He warmed to the end of his story. "When I brought Maren home, I did the right thing. I tried to find her mother's family, even hired a P.I. Six months and a hell of a lot of money later, the P.I. told me he couldn't find any trace of her. Maren's mother was a runaway no one apparently noticed was missing. So I gave Maren a family. Me."

Because his whole family was involved in either law enforcement or some branch of the law, Jared couldn't help thinking about the repercussions. "What about all the legal ramifications?"

Joe took another sip of his wine as he studied the man sitting beside him. "You really are a straight arrow, aren't you? I like that." And because he did, he gave Jared an honest answer. "Ramifications can be gotten around if you know the right people. Or the wrong people, depending on your take on the matter. But as far as Maren is concerned, she's my daughter and I'm her father." His smile brightened. "Having her in my life turned it around. I got a job, went to school nights, got a better job. And raised one hell of a great kid while I was at it." He reflected on his last words. "In a way, I guess we kind of raised each other."

Finished with stacking the dishes in the dishwasher, Maren picked that time to reenter the dining room. She gave Joe a reproving look.

"Papa, you're not boring him with that 'dark and stormy night' story, are you?"

"Did I mention it was raining that night?" Joe asked Jared, not bothering to hide his grin.

"You did now."

Jared sat back in his chair as Maren swept away the wineglasses after pausing to drain hers.

He'd enjoyed himself tonight, Jared thought. Really enjoyed himself. What's more, he felt pretty confident in thinking that neither Joe nor Maren had anything to do with any possible money laundering that might be going on at Rainbow's End. Over the course of the evening, he'd woven in enough leading questions so as to feel certain of their innocence.

According to Glassel, the background check on both hadn't turned up so much as a parking ticket between them. He was going to have to look elsewhere for evidence.

The thought heartened rather than annoyed him. Exploring why was best left for another time.

As Maren slipped back into her seat, Joe glanced at his watch. "Damn, how did it get to be so late already?"

Genuine disappointment outlined his features. "Shepherd wants me to come in early to the downtown branch tomorrow." He rose from the table, looking at Jared and Maren. "The two of you are welcome to hang around, talk to Tucker." He scratched the German shepherd's head.

"No." Rising to her feet, Maren said, "We might as well get going, too." Realizing she'd usurped him, she glanced at Jared for any contradiction. He nodded good-naturedly in response. The man was agreeable in all the right places, which wasn't good. He was causing her guard to slip, and she had to watch this. "I'll get your roasting pan and pots," she offered, beginning to walk back into the kitchen. "Just give me a minute to wash them out."

But Joe moved to block her exit. "I'll take care of that, Maren." He nodded toward Jared. "Jared here won't mind if I bring the cookware into the restaurant the next time I come into the office, right, Jared?" He thought a moment, although Jared got the impression the older man had already worked out all the details before he'd ever opened his mouth. "I could swing by tomorrow afternoon."

He knew his uncle wouldn't mind. The man had five of everything. "Fine with me."

"It's settled then," Joe said to Maren. "No washing pots and pans."

He escorted them both to the door, with Tucker prancing in front of all three, doing his best to act as a furry roadblock.

At the door, Maren sank down to her knees beside the animal, taking his face in her hands. "Sorry, Tuck, but I'll be back sooner this time, I promise. And the next time I come, we'll go to the park. How's that?"

As if in response, the dog licked her face and she laughed, rubbing his fur affectionately.

Jared looked on and marveled. Since he'd never had a pet himself, the firsthand connection between master and animal was untrod territory for him.

"He understands." The mild surprise he felt was evident in his voice.

"Sure he does," Joe told him. "Tucker knows he's a member of the family. He thinks he's human." And then he grinned as he looked at Maren. "That, and there might be a drop of sauce on her face. Don't know who enjoyed the duck more, us or Tucker."

About to get up, Maren became aware that Jared was offering her his hand. After a moment she took it. The fingers closed around hers, bringing her to her feet in a quick, sweeping motion. His hands were strong, reminding her of how safe she'd felt as a child. Back then she'd been confident that nothing could hurt her as long as she was in the magic circle of her father's arms.

Funny how things came back to you when you least expected them, she mused.

Jared saw the faraway look in her eyes as she rose to her feet. "Something wrong?"

"Just thinking." Shaking off her mood, she turned and kissed Joe on the cheek. "See you tomorrow maybe."

"Hope so." Joe accompanied them to the curb where the car was parked. He shook hands with his young visitor. "Thanks again, Jared, for a great meal. And anytime you want to go off on your own, open your own place, let me know."

The offer, coming out of left field, surprised him. "You're offering to be my accountant?" Jared asked.

"That, and maybe do a little investing. Be your silent partner. Be nice finally being involved with someone I liked…" Joe's voice trailed off. Then, as if he realized what he was saying, he shrugged away the moment. "Don't get me wrong, Jared. Shepherd's decent enough to work for."

"What about Rineholdt?" Jared pressed. They hadn't mentioned the other partner the entire evening. No one really mentioned him at the restaurant. And nothing had turned up on Glassel's end, either. It was as if the man was pure vapor. "I've never met the man," he said casually, then looked from Maren to Joe. "Have you?"

"Once," Joe admitted after a moment's reflection. "But he prefers being a silent partner. Likes leaving the business up to Shepherd and just counting the profits. Shepherd likes the limelight."

"That's the feeling I got," Jared admitted. Especially after what Maren had told him about the man.

Maren said nothing. Instead she got into the car. Taking his cue, Jared moved around the rear of the vehicle and got in on the driver's side.

Joe backed away from the car, pulling Tucker with

him. "Get going, you two, before we manage to talk away another hour out here."

Starting his car, Jared waved to the man as he pulled away from the curb.

Maren twisted against her seat belt, watching until both man and dog disappeared from view before she sat facing forward again. When she settled back against the seat, Jared had the impression she was tense again.

Why?

Chapter 10

He stood it as long as he could.

Eyes fixed on the road, Jared switched on the radio. A Rolling Stones's tune filled the interior of the vehicle, its lyrics largely indistinguishable. At least it chased away the silence that had been riding with them for the past five minutes.

He glanced at Maren for her reaction. Her expression gave nothing away. He gestured toward the radio. "Want to hear anything in particular?"

It took her a second to respond. "What?" She looked at the radio in the dashboard as if it had asked her the question, then belatedly shook her head. "No, anything's fine."

But everything was *not* fine. He was going through his own turbulence, but it helped somewhat to ask about hers. "Something wrong, Maren? You're a million miles away."

"Just lost in thought," she said, shrugging her shoulders. She wasn't lost, she was going around in circles, and he was right there in the center.

Was she thinking about the same thing he was? he wondered. About what was brewing between them? About the pull he'd felt, the pull that kept growing stronger?

"You should always leave markers," he said flippantly.

Maren turned toward him, confusion in her eyes. "What?"

"Markers," he repeated. "So you don't lose your way."

Inwardly she shook her head. *Too late for that.* She should have never agreed to come to dinner, not if Jared was going to be there. It was far too personal an experience, being in the home where she'd grown up. Being around the only man she'd ever thought of as family. Being there with a man who caused tidal waves in her soul.

"What if I lose the markers?" she asked.

He could certainly identify with that, Jared thought wryly. His own had somehow gotten covered in dust during the course of the evening. All he could think of was making love with her. He really needed to take a cold shower. Hell, maybe he'd just sit in his freezer for a while.

"Then I'd say you had a problem."

"Amen to that." It was an apt summation. She did have a problem, and the only way she knew how to handle it was with silence. Because the moment there was a dialogue going on between them, she found herself opening up to him. Found herself wanting to talk to him, to share.

Found herself just wanting to be with him.

And none of the flimsy excuses she kept feeding herself worked. She knew exactly what was going on. She was standing on quicksand and any second, it was going to swallow her up.

"Anything I can do to help?" he offered.

Other than disappearing off the face of the earth? Nope, 'fraid not. She tried very hard not to react to the kindly note in his voice. Why was he holding on to the steering wheel so tightly that his knuckles bulged?

"Thanks, but I'll work this out on my own."

He told himself to focus on the fact that he was still searching for evidence, that sometimes the most innocent of statements led to an eventual bust. But what he was feeling right now had nothing to do with money laundering, or evidence, and everything to do with the woman sitting here beside him in the dark.

"Sometimes it helps to have a sounding board," he heard himself say as he took another corner.

She knotted her hands in her lap, staring straight ahead. "And sometimes it doesn't."

"Ouch." Making another sharp right, he pulled into her complex. Slowly he made his way toward her block of apartments, searching for an empty space in guest parking. Finding one, he guided his vehicle into it. "I guess that puts me in my place."

Hardly. She unbuckled her seat belt then became aware that he was doing the same. Maren opened her door quickly. "You don't have to walk me to my door."

He got out on his side. "My mother taught me never to just drop a woman off in her front walk as if she were the morning newspaper."

She looked at him pointedly over the roof of the car. "Your mother's not here."

"No, but she left a lasting impression." Rounding the hood, he was at her side before she could take the next step.

She laughed shortly. "You know, in your own way, you're very pushy."

Taking her elbow, he began to walk her to her apartment. "I prefer the word determined. Gallant's not so bad, either."

About to shrug him off, she let it go instead. He'd be gone in a minute. No harm in the brief contact. "Is that what you're being? Gallant?"

He flashed a smile at her and she felt two salvos to either one of her knees. "See, there's so little of it these days you can't even recognize it when you come across it."

She started hunting for her key even before they reached her door. "Like chivalry, right?"

They walked past an apartment ablaze with lights and noise. Someone was having a party, and he caught himself thinking about having a party of his own. A party with only two people in attendance.

Mentally he began turning the faucet on for that cold shower he sorely needed. "Exactly."

After rounding a well-manicured corner populated with sleeping ice plants, Jared brought her closer to her door. With each step he took, he was acutely aware of the warring factions within him. On the one hand, he knew he should press his advantage, coax her to invite him in, perhaps even spend the night. Lovers told each other things that strangers didn't. He wasn't about to talk, but maybe she would. It wasn't that he suspected her of being involved in the crime, but that didn't mean she wasn't privy to knowledge that might help his investigation. Sometimes people didn't know what it was they knew.

On the other hand, because he felt things for her—deep, nebulous things he didn't want to examine too closely—a nobler part of him thought it would be best just to withdraw after making sure she was safely inside her apartment. A nobler part and a more private part. Making love with her would only complicate things, not facilitate them. In his heart, he knew that.

But it was his damn heart that kept getting in the way. He felt torn, doomed no matter which way he turned.

Nervous anticipation licked at her from all sides. She needed to slip into her apartment before something happened. Before she kissed him the way she'd been aching to all evening. There, she'd finally admitted it to herself. Her growing desire had been nagging at her the entire time she'd been at Papa Joe's. Every word she and Jared had exchanged, every look that had gone between them, had that urge behind it.

She wanted to make love with him. Wanted to feel him touching her. Wanting her. One would think after being all but bounced on her head by Kirk, she'd know better than to let herself be drawn to someone like Jared. *But,* a small voice inside her insisted, *Jared isn't anything like Kirk.* Except for his looks. But even there, he excelled.

"You're thinking again," he observed. "I can hear the wheels turning from here."

Facing him, the key still clutched tightly in her hand, Maren shrugged. "Sorry, occupational habit."

"You're thinking about the restaurant." The look in his eyes told her he knew better.

She held on to the lie as if it was her only lifeline in the middle of shark-infested waters. Even though it was quickly dissolving.

"Yes."

The smile spread slowly, starting in his eyes and finding its way to his lips. "You're not much of a liar, Maren Minnesota."

About to protest, she gave it up before the words saw the light of day. "I don't get much practice."

"That's good." The softly whispered words hung between them in the night air. "Honesty is a very sexy quality in a woman."

"Just in a woman?" she breathed.

"Especially in a woman," he qualified.

Giving in, yet still struggling to hold a tight rein on himself, Jared brushed a soft kiss against her hair. He had no way of knowing that it was the fastest way of melting the icy reserve she was attempting to surround herself with.

"Lying leaves a bad taste in your mouth," he told her.

She tilted her head up to look into his eyes. She felt as if her entire being vibrated with anticipation. "Speaking from experience?"

He moved his head from side to side slowly, his eyes never leaving hers. "From hearsay."

She wanted to believe him, believe in the moment, believe in the purity of what was happening here between them. But she was afraid. Afraid of getting burned again.

Yet she couldn't make herself retreat. "And is that a lie, too?"

"You make me want to do things, Maren." He framed her face in his hands, his heart speeding up and beating wildly in his chest. "Wild, insane things."

She could feel her breath backing up in her lungs. Every sane bone in her body begged her to run for cover. But she wasn't listening to sanity, she was listening to the rush of desire as it overtook her veins.

"Such as?"

He didn't want words any longer. He wanted her.

Jared lowered his mouth to hers and kissed her. Kissed her long and hard. The restraint he'd been holding on to so tightly splintered completely, falling through his fingers like so many tiny toothpicks.

He enveloped her in his arms and deepened the kiss. Deepened so that it dragged him down into its center, threatening to never release him. He didn't care. As long as he could go down with Maren.

Jared held her closer, tighter, trying to satisfy his growing hunger with the feel of her body pressed against his. He told himself it was enough, but this was just as much of a lie as the ones he'd told her.

The attempt to sate himself backfired, only making him hungrier. Noble thoughts fled like so many leaves in the autumn wind, to be replaced with desire that thundered through his entire being.

A rush swept through her so quickly, it snatched her breath away. The promises she'd made to herself, even seconds ago, shattered, not one by one, but in unison, sending a tidal wave of demands and urges through her. Ever since Kirk had walked out on her, she'd been completely celibate. She hadn't even been tempted so much as once.

Until Jared had walked into her office.

Now she couldn't think of anything else, of anyone else. Only of being with him in every way. She could barely breathe when he pulled away. Her heart hammered so hard, it felt as if it was going to fly out of her throat at any second.

"Oh," she finally managed to murmur, remembering that he'd said something about wanting to do insane things an eternity ago. "You mean those kinds of things."

He had one chance. One chance to be noble, before he begged her to let him stay. But even as he tried to take it, he was still holding her. Still feeling the current that had swept through him.

"I'd better go."

"No."

Maren had whispered the word so softly, he was sure it was his own imagination that had given voice to the entreaty.

Until she added, "Don't."

He took hold of her hands, bringing each to his lips and kissing them one at a time. Everything inside him wanted to agree. But he knew she was vulnerable, knew he'd be taking advantage of that. Knew, too, that he was just as needy in his own way as she was.

For the first time in his life, he wanted someone. Wanted a woman not just with his body, but with something else. With a need that made him suddenly aware of the large gaping hole in his soul. A hole he'd never been aware of before.

The war within him upped the stakes. "You don't know what you're asking, Maren."

Her eyes never left his. Beyond the need, he saw a strength there and it surprised him. And yet, it was what he liked about her. She was her own woman. Problem was, he wanted her to be *his* woman.

"I'm not some wide-eyed innocent, Jared. I know what I'm asking."

He framed her face again and brought his mouth

down to hers once more. He meant only to brush his lips against hers. Meant to kiss her goodbye, not kiss his own strength goodbye.

But it was inevitable. The more he kissed her, the more he wanted to kiss her. The more he wanted to be with her. His need grew bigger than his resolve.

"Maren?" he murmured against her lips.

"Hmm?"

"Maybe you'd better unlock your door before the neighbors call the police."

He felt her mouth curve into a smile against his mouth. Saw both the anticipation and promise of pleasure in her eyes just before she turned to insert the key she'd been clutching into the lock. A quick twist and they were inside.

Alone with the shadows of their pasts.

Jared pushed the door closed behind him and the darkness swallowed them up. As did the passion that was raging within both of them. He kissed her over and over again. Kissed her as his hands jerked off first her coat then the pullover blouse she'd worn. His fingers searched for the snap at her waist to loosen the little navy skirt she'd put on mere hours ago. The one that had been driving him crazy with each and every step she'd taken.

As he pushed the fabric down the tantalizing swell of her hips, his fingers brushed against a small scrap of material. He heard her sharp intake of breath as he followed the outline along her buttocks and then toward the very core of her. Her belly quivered against his fingers. He was versed enough to know that she wore a thong.

The image that conjured up in his mind was enough to put him in danger of swallowing his own tongue.

She'd followed his lead, frantic movement for frantic movement. Divesting him of his jacket, his shirt, his pants. The hunger she discovered burning within her had changed her. She'd never felt this level of anticipation, this level of eagerness before. It was as if she was going to explode if she didn't make love with him. She couldn't hope to control what she was experiencing. She could only let herself be swept away by it.

The feel of his hands along her body heated her so that she was certain she was going to ignite right here right at the door inside her small apartment. Her body moistened as he plundered its secrets with his hands, his mouth, his tongue.

Drawing the very essence of her soul from her. Replacing it with heat, with lights, with a rush so overwhelming and overpowering she didn't have a prayer of surviving.

Her world was tilting.

The next second she realized that Jared had brought her down to the floor, right here on the soft pile created by their abandoned clothes.

Hands laced through hers, he assaulted her skin with his mouth. She twisted and turned against him, absorbing every sensation, reveling in it. He was making her indelibly his as he kissed, teased, branded every inch of her.

As he slid his tongue along her belly, she felt every muscle quiver involuntarily.

Felt her core growing damp for wanting him.

And the dampness was heating. Heating as his mouth found her. Tantalized her. She cried out as the sensations grew more powerful. It was as if a giant wave was coming for her, threatening to drown her.

And still, she rushed toward it. Anticipating it.

She bucked, arched, tightened her legs around him as the climax he'd created took possession of her, racking her body.

Growing.

One explosion flowered into another like a majestic display of Fourth of July fireworks. And then the sensation ebbed away. Exhaustion pressed down on her. Exhaustion that mysteriously vanished the instant he began to slide his body over hers.

She felt his desire hard against her. Pressing her lips together, she spread her legs apart and invited him to join with her.

His eyes held her prisoner.

And then he was inside her. Moving slowly, then with more and more pent-up energy. She couldn't have remained passive if she'd wanted to. Energy came from somewhere, meeting the rhythm of his body. Urging it further.

He locked his hands with hers again. Moving so that the room, the very world, began to spin around her, making her airborne.

And when the final sensation came for him, Jared gathered her to him, holding her tightly, as if the two of them were hurtling down a chasm and all he could do to save her was shield her with his own body. The words were born in that heat, in that instant, escaping his lips without escort. Without thought. "I love you."

When the final moment came to her, Maren thought she heard him murmur something against her ear. The sound buzzed in her head as the explosion she'd been anticipating echoed through her body, shaking it down to its very core.

The euphoria seized her, holding her tightly, as tightly as his arms were wrapped around her. Even now, in its full grip, she mourned the second when the euphoria would pass. But for the moment, she savored it as long as she could. Wishing with all her soul that it could somehow last forever.

She felt his body begin to relax against her, felt his hold loosen ever so slightly until it went lax altogether.

And then Jared was over her, pivoting himself on his elbows, lightly moving her damp hair from her cheek. His eyes telling her things in the enduring silence that hummed between them.

An almost unbearable sweetness seized her.

Softly, he kissed her. Kissed her as if they hadn't just made wild, passionate love on her floor. Kissed her as if they were only two very young people on the brink of the mysteries of first love.

Her heart whispered something to her she was afraid

to hear. Afraid because she knew it wouldn't turn out to be true.

She made him care. Really, really care. And that had never happened before. Had he been in his right mind, he would have been scared to death. But that was all for later. Right now, he wanted to enjoy the moment, to savor it because he instinctively knew it couldn't possibly be like this again.

Finally her voice returned to her and, with it, some semblance of normal breathing. "Did you say something before?"

Self-preservation had him erasing the moment from his mind. Almost. He glided the back of his hand along her cheek. "When?"

He was doing it to her again. Making her want him. Making her feel like some schoolgirl with her first crush. "Just now," she said with effort. "Just before you, um—"

They'd just made love like two wild, abandoned souls and now she sounded like some shy virgin who'd just been deflowered. Something wrapped itself around his heart and he knew he was powerless against it.

He tried to be flippant and didn't quite pull it off. "Maybe 'thank you.' I'm not sure," he added. "I was a little out of my head." Lying beside her, he pulled her to him, content not to move for the moment. "Did I mention that you were magnificent?"

He could feel her smiling against his chest. Could feel the warmth that generated within his soul.

"No."

"I should have. You were." He kissed the top of her head and smiled to himself. The darkness had abated as his eyes had grown accustomed to it. He could make things out now. Thing like the door. "You realize we didn't make it five feet into the apartment?"

"That much?" Unable to help herself, she began to draw patterns on his chest with her fingertip. He had a light smattering of hair, just enough to tantalize her.

"Don't do that," he warned quietly.

She didn't understand. "Why not?"

"Because then I might do this." Rising up on one elbow, he leaned over her. The kiss that followed had her throbbing all over again.

"I'll take my chances," she said breathlessly, kissing him back and starting the dance all over again.

Chapter 11

"Don't think I don't know what you're doing."

Jared looked up in surprise as Max snarled the words in his ear, loud enough only for him to hear. The other man had whispered despite the fact that the kitchen was deserted. The rest of the kitchen staff was taking their morning break.

"Making Hungarian goulash," Jared answered automatically. He looked back at the dish he was preparing. It was new on the menu and, per request, he'd made a sample for Maren to taste.

Max moved his considerable bulk in front of Jared, forcing him to stop and look at him. "Don't get smart with me, pretty boy. I mean the other thing."

"Other thing?" Jared wiped his hands on his apron and gave Max his full attention. Mentally bracing himself. "What 'other thing'?"

Not a handsome man to begin with, Max was a shade removed from ugly when he scowled.

"You know what I'm talking about. Cozying up to Maren." His eyes were dark, piercing and malevolent, like those of an ogre protecting his territory. "That's not going to get you anywhere. I'm head chef here and I'm planning on staying that way."

Jared sighed. The man was putting his own spin on events, seeing him as a threat. That wasn't the way to go about an investigation.

"I'm not after your job, Max," he told the head chef patiently. "This isn't *All About Eve*."

Though a good fifteen years older, Max obviously hadn't a clue what he was talking about.

"Huh?"

"It's an old movie, Max. I caught it on one of those classic channels the other night. Newbie wheedles her way into a star's entourage. Quietly goes about weaving her way into a place of power. Winds up stabbing her mentor in the back and taking over her role."

Max's expression indicated that was *exactly* what he thought the new assistant chef was doing. Jared slipped an arm around the man's wide shoulders, trying to subtly convey a note of friendship.

"First of all, I'm not a newbie. I know my way around a kitchen, have for a very long time." The kitchen in question was his uncle's but there was no point in mentioning that. "Second, you're not my mentor, although I'm more than willing to learn from you. And third, I'm happy doing what I'm doing."

The sneer was still there. "By doing the manager?" Max asked.

Jared removed his arm from the man's shoulders. Something dark stirred inside of him, an anger that he rarely encountered. A steely look came into Jared's eyes as he turned to face Max. The affable aura he'd maintained since he'd first arrived on the job vanished like vapor. "You've got to the count of five to apologize for that."

Clearly uncertain, Max tried to maintain his position. "And if I don't?"

Silence met Max's question and then Jared said in a low, controlled voice that had made more than one perp's blood run cold, "Trust me, you don't want an answer to that question."

Max had fifty pounds on Jared, but self-preservation made the man realize that while the poundage he was carrying around was just weight, what Jared had on him was solid muscle.

Amid glares, Max backed off. "Okay, I'm sorry I insulted you."

"Not me, Maren," Jared told him evenly. But to a casual passer-by, there was no mistaking the threat behind the words.

With a huff Max held his hands up, as if physically

pushing away both Jared and the words that had gone between them. "Okay, okay. I just got mad, okay?" the man exclaimed. "I didn't mean to insult her. I like Maren. She's a decent person." Unable to curb himself, he added, "You, I'm not so sure about yet." Uneasy, he took another step back, his hands still raised. "But hey, all I know from is cooking."

Turning tail, Max quickly went to join the others who were clustered outside. He didn't even stop to take his jacket. It was only after the man had disappeared that the smattering of applause came from behind him.

Jared turned to see that Joe had been watching the latter part of the exchange from the alcove that led to the ground-level pantry.

"Nice display of chivalry," the man commented, coming forward. "Maren would have appreciated it if she'd heard you."

Maren wouldn't have appreciated the nature of the exchange in the first place, Jared thought.

"Maren would have put him in his place herself if she'd heard. I was just acting on her behalf," Jared said, wondering what was going on in the accountant's mind. Did Joe suspect that he was sleeping with his daughter?

The two men looked at one another for a long moment and Jared had the impression that he was being sized up—really sized up. Far more intently than he had been the other night at Joe's house. Was the man seeing him as a potential match for Maren? Or was there something else on Joe's mind?

Just when he'd made up his mind to absolve both the accountant and Maren of having any connections to this money laundering case he was trying to break, nagging doubts crept in again, setting everything on its ear.

That was why he was good at his job, he supposed. He never ruled anything out a hundred percent until he was absolutely convinced he was making the right decision.

Joe's expression softened. "Good to know Maren's got someone looking out for her." Joe paused a moment, as if weighing what he was going to say next. "She's not the easiest woman to get to know," he admitted, though there was a fond albeit sad note in his voice. "I'm surprised she's as well adjusted as she is, considering what she's had to put up with."

There was just the two of them in the kitchen. Otherwise he would have never said what he said next. "You mean, about her baby dying?"

Mild surprise registered on Joe's face. Jared had the impression that nothing ever completely rattled the older man. But this, he had a hunch, had come close in its time.

"She told you about that?"

Jared nodded. "Yeah."

The mild surprise gave way to a look that was somewhat pleased. Jared wasn't certain just how to interpret that. "She must trust you more than I thought. No one else knows about Melissa except me."

His tone left things unsaid. That Maren hadn't been

the only one who had taken the baby's death hard. After all, the baby had been his grandchild in every way except blood.

The fact that he'd been allowed into this small, intimate circle made Jared feel that much more guilty about the lies he was telling these people, necessary or not. People didn't suffer liars well, even if it was for a noble end.

It had been three days since he'd made love with Maren. Three days in which they'd politely acknowledged one another when their paths crossed at the restaurant, but she had for the most part kept away from him. Part of that, he knew, was caused by the fact that the manager at the other restaurant had suddenly quit, leaving the people over there in a lurch. Rather than stepping in himself, Shepherd had asked her to oversee things there as well as here.

In a way, Jared took the forced separation as a respite. He needed time to pull himself together, time to process what had happened and to be able to weave it into the framework he was operating in. He couldn't neutralize the effects of the event when part of his brain was continually preoccupied with thoughts of her. With fantasizing about making love with her again.

He knew that it would be to his advantage to pretend to be involved with Maren. It could deepen his cover, make him more a part of the restaurant's inner circle. But by the same token, the deception he was forced to weave would leave that much more of a scar on Maren once she knew who he really was and what he was really doing here.

But "Jared Stevens" would press his advantage with Maren, he told himself. That was the persona he'd created—a Romeo.

Not completely unlike himself, Jared thought ruefully.

"She needs someone like you, Jared," Joe said to him. "To make her forget about the past and live again. Twenty-seven is much too young to think that there's nothing more to life than working." Joe paused again, as if deciding whether or not to intrude further. "Why don't you give her a call tonight?" he suggested with a broad smile.

Jared decided to take it as a sign to move in that direction. For the good of the case. "Maybe I will."

Joe nodded, pleased. "Just don't let her know I said so," he added with a wink as he walked back into his office.

The person he needed to nail down was Warren Shepherd, Jared thought that evening as he slipped into the empty office Maren shared with her father. Not an easy thing. The man moved from one restaurant to the other without any set pattern or predictability.

A tail had been out on him, and Weissman, the policeman assigned to the job, had seen Shepherd meeting with the Mafia lieutenant, Gaspare Rosetti, at the other restaurant. The meeting wasn't very much to go on, falling under the heading of circumstantial evidence. After all, the two had been friends since the early days of their boyhood. During the meeting, Weissman said that no amount of money had even crossed hands because Shepherd had refused to allow the other man to pay for his meal. At the end of the meal, the two had embraced and then Rosetti had gone his own way.

It wasn't a crime to embrace. Unless money had been slipped from one pocket to the other, Jared had suddenly thought. When he'd suggested it to Weissman, the latter had admitted that he hadn't paid that close attention to the exchange of affectionate respect. So it was a possibility. A little sleight of hand and who knew how much "richer" Shepherd's establishment was? Temporarily.

If money had crossed hands, at the very least there might be an influx of investor funds showing up on books to coincide with that. But to ascertain that, he needed to get a look at Joe's computer.

The accountant had left to go to the other branch shortly after their exchange over Max's less than chivalrous comments. Maren was already there. Added to that, Shepherd never showed up at this time of day. Opportunity was quietly knocking, Jared told himself. For a very short period of time.

He had fifteen minutes to get in and out when the others went on their respective evening breaks.

Jared never hesitated.

Rather than turn on Joe's computer, he decided that

maybe he might be able to find something on Maren's. The two new stoves and mashed potato machine that had just arrived yesterday had to have invoices from somewhere. He wanted to match up the prices to the information that was ultimately on Joe's spreadsheets. Besides, at Maren's desk he'd be facing the door, not having his back to it. No one could sneak up on him from behind.

The moment he turned on Maren's computer, his conscience began to give him trouble. He did his best to ignore it. Conscience was a luxury he couldn't afford right now. Finding her password was a matter of allowing the department's new electronic gadget to do its work.

Five seconds later, he was in.

Detaching the hand-held apparatus from the USB connection, he dumped it and its connector into its small black carrying case and went to work.

Less than a minute later, he froze.

He heard Maren's voice coming from down the hall. She was talking to April. The other woman's voice was impossible to miss. Maren was asking her how she felt. The salad girl had taken a couple days off when an infection had set in on her finger. But she was better now, she told Maren.

He could testify to that. The small, plucky blonde was hitting on him again.

As coolly as a career solider finding himself under enemy fire, Jared quickly closed down Maren's computer.

The soft, telltale hum peculiar to that computer had just that second died away and he was about to rise from the desk when Maren opened the door. He quickly began rifling through things. With his toe, he moved the small black case out if sight behind her trash basket.

Maren stopped dead, staring at him. He was the last person she'd expected to find in here, especially in the dark.

She flipped on the light switch. The fluorescent bulbs overhead came to life, casting light everywhere. It didn't help to illuminate her. Slowly she closed the door behind her, wondering if she should leave it open. But no, Jared wasn't dangerous. She would stake her life on that. "What are you doing here?"

His expression was the soul of innocence as he guilelessly explained, "Looking for a piece of paper to leave you a note."

"A note?" She dropped her purse on her desk and looked at him. "Why didn't you just call me on my cell?" She knew he had the number since he'd used it to keep himself from turning into an ice pop.

"Note writing's a lost art, don't you think?" Putting down the pen he'd just snatched up on her entrance, he leaned over to kiss her. Maren pulled back. He looked at her for a moment, unable to read what was going on in her mind. "Part of the note was going to be about that."

Starting to say something, she stopped and cocked her head. He's managed to catch her off guard. Again. "About what?"

"About avoiding me." When he moved into her space, he was gratified that she didn't immediately back away. That came after a second's thought. But it did come. He shook his head. "I thought we had a break-through the other night."

She was desperately trying to separate herself from the events of the other night. To put distance between herself and the feelings that kept threatening to jump up at her like some jack-in-the-box whose lid was poorly secured.

"We slept together. That's not a breakthrough."

"It is in some books and I'd hardly call what we did sleeping." The wicked grin abated and softened. "Joe likes me."

Maren waved that off. She placed her hand on the monitor as she talked. It felt mildly warm, the way it did when it was in the process of being turned on. Was it malfunctioning?

"Joe likes everyone." And then she paused as his words replayed themselves in her head. "Why, did he say something to you?"

He was doing his best to distract her. But telling himself he was just playing a part no longer carried any weight. He knew he was getting hopelessly tangled up in the woman he was lying to. "He thought I might be good for you, get you to forget about work for a while."

Maren sighed, weary on all fronts. These last few days had been hard on her, juggling two positions and one set of emotions that had gone amuck. "I've got twice as much work to forget about now."

He lent her a sympathetic ear. "No luck finding a new manager for the other branch?"

She shook her head. But the matter was far more complicated that just finding a replacement for the idiot who had abruptly left.

"The whole structure over there needs to be revamped." For a second she hesitated, as if telling tales out of school. But then, she'd never really felt any allegiance to the man who had hired both Papa Joe and her. As far as she was concerned, in both cases he'd gotten far more than he was paying for. She often thought the man took advantage of Joe.

"Shepherd put in someone from his family there, a nephew who thought the place could run itself. It couldn't. Added to that, the nephew was skimming off the top. There's a cash flow problem now."

"Where is this nephew now?" he asked casually.

"Nobody knows. He's just disappeared with the money, we assume. Shepherd's fit to be tied. I've never seen him this upset before."

Jared could well imagine. If his nephew was skimming from the top somehow, there was no doubt that the man's disappearance could be traced to a sudden fondness for sleeping with fish. No wonder Shepherd was nervous, especially if he'd brought the man in to begin with.

"He says Rineholdt is lining up another investor to help out," she said.

"Ah, the mysterious Rineholdt." He was seriously beginning to think Rineholdt was an alias for Rosetti. It made sense. "Any chance of ever meeting him?"

The question pulled her out of her thoughts. She stared at him. "Why would you want to meet him?"

He shrugged casually. "Nice to know who I'm working for." And it would either validate or dispel his theory.

She pushed the matter aside. "As far as you're concerned, you're working for me."

He grinned, surprising her by taking her into his arms. "Love it when you get tough like that." But when he lowered his lips to hers, she turned her head, giving him a mouthful of hair.

She pulled free, but not before allowing herself to enjoy the moment fleetingly. "Jared, I can't kiss you here."

He gave her a look that went a long way to melting her knees. "Why?"

Just in case, she placed her hands on the back of her chair for support. "Because we're at work."

"Not me." He took a step toward her, his eyes teasing her. The expression on her face told him he had the upper hand no matter what she claimed to the contrary. He closed the door to the office. "I'm on a break, writing a note to the most fabulous woman I've ever been with."

This time when he took her into his arms, she didn't wiggle free. "Do you lay sauce on that thickly when you cook?"

"Every situation has to be evaluated separately," he told her seriously. And then his eyes smiled at her. "And I'm not laying anything on thickly. If anything, I'm understating it."

Unable to hold himself in check any longer, he kissed her. Not with the passion he felt, but with the affection that was entirely new to him. And as thrilling as it was scary.

It was hard for her not to sigh as she kissed him back and felt everything inside of her stand at attention. And beg for more. With effort, she pulled back, knowing if she didn't, she was going to melt against this man right here. "What was it about?"

"What was what about?" The question floated out on the wings of a contented sigh Maren vainly tried to suppress.

"Your note." It took effort to pull her thoughts together so that they made sense. "You said you were leaving me a note."

He slid his tongue along his lips, tasting her. Wanting her. Damn but she'd turned him inside out without any effort at all, he thought. What a time for this to happen, to meet a woman he'd want to spend time with, real time. But everything was in the way. He forced himself to focus on what was necessary. "Right. I was going to ask if you wanted to take in a late movie tonight."

The sweetness of what he said clashed with common sense, something she knew he had in abundance. Something she normally had in abundance. But not right now. "And if I didn't come in to see the note?"

He never hesitated. "I would have hand-delivered it to your place."

She laughed, shaking her head. Loving the feel of his arms around her. "You've got an answer for everything, don't you?"

He pretended to look at her with innocence. "Just the truth."

God, but he was so appealing. She was having more and more trouble resisting him. The roadblocks she put up kept getting flattened. Maren wrestled with her thoughts, knowing that if she took a step forward in this relationship, she would ultimately be taking a step back. Back into a place where she might not be able to work her way out of. And she was scared.

But Joe had given Jared his seal of approval. Even if Jared hadn't said anything just now, she could tell by the conversation at Joe's house the other night. Both men seemed to be feeling each other out, although Joe was far more intent on extracting information out of him than Jared had been. The very fact that Joe hadn't issued any warnings spoke volumes. Joe had never liked Kirk, had warned her that the man was only trouble. It was his inherent instinct had warned him since Kirk had been polite enough around him the two times the men had been in one another's company.

Joe's approval meant a lot to her but she was still afraid.

Damn it, are you going to live your entire life like a rabbit? You deserve some happiness and he's offering it to you.

She looked up at him, lacing her arms around his neck. "Tell you what, why don't we skip the movie and just go to your place?"

"My place?" She'd caught him off guard with that one. He was living in a motel right now, keeping well away from anything that tied him with his real life. He'd told her he was living in an apartment.

"Sure." Closing her eyes, she took in the scent of his cologne. And felt her pulse accelerate just the tiniest bit. "I'm curious about where you live."

"It's mess." He kissed the top of her head. "You'll find out what a slob I am."

"You? You have every utensil, every ingredient in its place. You put Max to shame." She suddenly remembered what had been on her mind when she'd come into the office. "Speaking of which, maybe I have a proposition for you."

Jared played on his advantage, knowing that he could distract Maren. Hating himself for using it as a tool. He brought his mouth close to hers, tantalizing her with his nearness. He kissed her neck softly. "Does it involve getting naked?"

"Only if you like to live dangerously," she said with effort. As he pulled back to look at her, her eyes were laughing at him. "Spilling something on yourself might really hurt then."

"I have a feeling we're not talking about the same thing."

She shook her head, doing her best not to laugh at

him. "I'm talking about taking over as head chef in the other branch."

He smiled at her wickedly. "I'm not." He brought his mouth back down to hers.

Talk of work, of changes, was temporarily tabled for the time being.

Chapter 12

Jared drove his vintage Mustang into Maren's apartment complex less than two car lengths directly behind Maren's light blue coupe. He parked in the first space he came across, going for availability rather than proximity. It was located a distance away from Maren's own reserved spot. Getting out, he quickened his pace, reaching her just as she was closing the door to her vehicle.

She looked so beautiful in the light of the full moon, something twisted inside him. Once again, he felt that same wonder, that same uneasiness. It unnerved him that he'd never felt this way about a woman before.

"Sure you don't want to take in a movie?" he teased.

"There's a preview showing after the main feature at the Sundown Megaplex, less than a mile away."

Rather than answer him, Maren wrapped her arms around his neck, brought her body in close to his and kissed him as if she'd set her cap on breaking some kind of an endurance record. The distance she'd been trying to maintain between them had clearly become a thing of the past.

At least for now.

His breath was completely depleted by the time the kiss ended. It took him a moment to suck air back into his lungs. "Guess not," he surmised. He smiled down into her face, feeling elated and like the lowest form of life all at the same time.

Still holding her keys, Maren took hold of his hand with her other one and led him from her parking space to her front door.

"Why, Ms. Minnesota," he murmured against her hair, breathing in the scent of her shampoo, knowing he was never going to feel the same way about magnolias again, "this is so sudden."

He was teasing her, she thought, but he'd struck a chord. It *was* sudden. Very sudden. She'd gone from passive to passionate in a little more time than it took Max to create the perfect soufflé.

But all this emotion had been waiting behind a locked door for such a long time.

As she watched Jared she realized that it wasn't in her never to love again. She needed the emotion dwelling within her. Holding herself in check the way she had all this time had been worse than hard for her. It had been torture.

And so was the fear of having to let go. The fear of what would happen if she let go. But this man made her feel as if he was going to be here for the duration. As if she could make plans with him, dream dreams and try to make them come true.

He made her feel like taking risks, yet made her feel safe all at the same time. Maren knew that she had no logical explanation for it, but then, at bottom, feelings could rarely be dissected to their smallest particle and still make sense. She was happy just to feel, just to be alive again.

Guilt ensnared him because the look in her eyes was one he'd seen before. It was the look of a woman about to give her heart away.

To a man who didn't exist.

To a man he'd made her believe existed. Once she knew the truth, was she going to hate him with the same passion she now felt?

He didn't want to know the answer, was afraid of knowing the answer.

With superhuman effort, Jared pushed away his negative thoughts. Like the man he'd created for this moment, he pretended tomorrow didn't exist. Consequences didn't exist. All that existed was this overwhelming desire that beat frantic wings within him. The desire to hold her, to have her. To make love with her.

And, if he was very, very lucky, to expire in her arms sometime during the night so that no consequences could ever be faced.

He wanted the evening to last. He wanted to place stars in her eyes and to make those last, as well. He wanted to give her beautiful memories so that when she looked back, she'd see that it hadn't been all bad between them. They'd had good times no matter what kind of a lowlife she would eventually believe him to be.

So, rather than undress her to the beat of the *Minute Waltz* the way he wanted to, Jared separated her from her clothes slowly. Moving aside her coat from her arms until it slid to the floor, he began to work the tiny buttons that ran along the length of her blouse. He could literally feel her chest heaving as he coaxed each button from its hole, skimming the tips of his fingers against the skin that was exposed as he worked his way down.

When the last button had been freed, he slowly dragged rather than pulled the sleeves from her arms, pausing to lightly press a kiss to each newly exposed area. It served to excite not only her, but him, as well.

Jared could feel her heart pounding beneath the lace of her bra as the blouse finally floated to the floor. He lightly brushed just the tip of his tongue along the swell of each breast.

"Are you out to make me crazy?" The question echoed in the darkness. He'd left the lights off. Her voice was low, raspy, as if every part of her was filled with needs, with demands.

"You did it to me first."

The whispered words gliding along her skin, making her belly tighten, making her loins moisten in anticipation. As she moved to open the clasp at the back of her bra, he stopped her. The look in his eyes told her that he wanted to do the honors himself.

She took a deep breath as the material loosened then slid from her breasts, lingering for a moment on her swollen nipples before he pulled it aside.

The passion in his eyes heated her. Made her feel beautiful.

Made her feel hungry for him.

She realized that she'd stood here, absorbing it all, forgetting to do anything herself. He'd made her completely weak, made her arms feel heavy, her fingers feel clumsy. It took effort to make them obey her as she pressed them into service.

Dragging a ragged breath into her lungs, she began to undress him even as he continued divesting her of her clothing. Maren pulled his jacket and shirt from him quickly, eagerly.

But when it came to his trousers, she began to follow his lead. Wanting to send the electricity she was experiencing into his limbs. So rather than unbutton, unzip and tug the material away, she did it slowly, allowing her fingers to languidly slip along the outline of his firm thighs, dragging her palm ever so lightly along the outline of his hardening desire.

She saw the heat leap into his eyes, felt the same sort

of heat emanate through his trousers. Felt the power that gave her. Her smile was slow, confident, as it slipped over her lips. Her eyes held his as she ran her fingers along the length of him before finally taking the zipper and pulling it down.

She cupped him just as his hand went between her legs, finding her softest core. Stroking her until she wanted to grab him by the shoulders with both hands and beg him to finish what he'd begun.

He did.

But he did it in his own time. Making time stand still and then catch fire.

Determined not to take her on the floor the way he had the first time, Jared led her into the small living room. The sofa bore witness to the rest of their love-making. Heard her cry out his name with anticipation, with joy, as he inserted his tongue where his fingers had been only moments ago. Bringing her to the brink of the highest peak, then taking her over it.

Explosion seized her body and she embraced him, searching for more, afraid that more would push her completely out her head. Exhausted, she fell back, try-ing to gather herself together. Only to discover that there was no respite. He was relentless in his need for her.

Another explosion, fiercer, wilder, blossomed in the wake of the first. And then, when she was certain that there was nothing left to feel, Jared proved her wrong. He moved until he was on top of her, pivoting so that the only weight she felt was what he wanted her to feel. Balanced, he plunged into her.

With a cry, she arched, wrapping her legs around him. Moving with him as if the very sofa was on fire. Just the way they were.

When he finally experienced the ultimate sensation, he held her to him as if he was never going to let her go. Wishing that he didn't have to.

"Next time," he whispered, his voice muffled against the side of her neck, "we'll make it to the bed."

Next time. He was making plans. Plans that included her. There was something beyond tonight. Maren smiled against his shoulder, planting small, butterfly kisses along his skin. "Oh, good, something to live for."

Jared forced himself up on his elbows. Forced himself to look at her. She'd just made love with him. Made love to a man she thought was a simple chef. She had no way of knowing he was living a lie. That he was really an undercover detective sent to spy on her, on her father, her place of work. On the people she regarded as friends.

Words filled his throat, begging to be released.

He'd never felt the urge for confession before. He did now. It beat at him with small, clenched fists, demanding release. But this wasn't his secret to tell. A great deal of time and effort had gone into setting this up and if it was true, if the restaurants were fronts for laundering mob money, who knew how far this web extended and who they would bring down once they had what they needed?

He was a cop, damn it. This was what he was trained for. Which meant that he didn't have the luxury of telling her.

And better that he didn't. Because the moment he told her who he really was, what he was really doing here, it would be over between them.

He wasn't ready for it to be over.

Jared lightly kissed her lips. "Well, that was good for starters," he told her. His eyes teased her. "When are you planning on bringing out the heavy artillery?"

She laughed and he could feel the vibrations all along his body. "Think you could stand it?"

"Why don't we try it and see?"

She brought her arms up around his neck, pulling him down to her. "Your wish is my command."

He let his mind go blank as he made love with her again.

Within the next few days, Jared made a fascinating discovery. Rather than slip into the red because of mismanagement, the total accounts of Rainbow's End were so far into the black, Shepherd had more equipment brought into both branches. The remainder of the old ranges were replaced with models that cooked faster and accommodated more pots and pans at the same time.

They also came with huge price tags.

"Nothing but the best for my place," Shepherd was heard to say.

According to word of mouth, profits continued to grow, making unseen, unknown investors richer.

Jared felt itchy. He needed to get into Joe's computer. He had a hunch he might find something there that would lead him to a second set of books. The old embezzlement expression "cooking the books" would never be more appropriate than here, he thought grimly.

But in order to find anything of worth out, he needed Joe's password. Not the password that initially unlocked the computer, but a second one that defied any method of detection.

The software the accountant was using was like one he'd never seen before. It demanded a password within a password. The program was, despite the latest equipment he had at his disposal, impossible to hack into in the limited amount of time he had. He needed Joe's help, especially now since the body of the former assistant chef, Emil, who had initially come to them about the money laundering, had washed ashore.

Any doubts Jared had harbored about the case were gone.

But despite what he felt in his gut about Joe Collins, he couldn't very well approach the man unprepared, with nothing to offer for his help. If Joe turned out to be involved somehow, approaching him would lead to a domino effect, sending the news to those at the top. He needed to have something to offer the accountant in exchange for his help.

And he couldn't make the offer in good faith on his own. He hadn't the authority.

So before he could approach Joe for his help, he needed another kind of help. Legal help.

He was familiar with the customary route and it yielded nothing but frustration. Going through channels meant getting involved in red tape. Miles of red tape. And it took time. He hadn't the patience for the former and there wasn't all that much of the latter available. He'd already been informed that the funds behind this investigation were going to dry up if he didn't come up with something soon.

When he called the restaurant to say that he'd be late Joe answered. "Anything wrong?"

Jared thought fast. "No, just a kid sister with a problem. I promise I'll be in before the doors open."

"Don't worry, just take care of what you need to take care of. Most important thing in the world is family, Jared. When you get to be my age, you'll appreciate that."

"I already do."

Damn, but he felt guilty, Jared thought, closing his cell phone. Guilty even though he was only half lying. He was going to see his sister, but she wasn't the one with a problem.

He was.

Janelle Cavanaugh looked like all the Cavanaugh women, except for her cousin Patience. Patience was the only redhead in the lot. The others took after their paternal grandmother. They were all light to golden blond, with high cheekbones and slender figures that curved in all the right places.

Because they were so close in age, he'd been extremely protective of Janelle when they were growing up. Protective and antagonistic at the same time. They'd fought like cats and dogs and presented a united front to the rest of the world the way only a brother and sister could.

At times, he had trouble convincing himself that she wasn't that quick-fisted tomboy who could sucker punch him time and again anymore, but a capable young woman the D.A. had made favorable references to in a press conference more than once.

He'd come to see her in that capacity now.

Janelle swept into the room, dressed in a no-nonsense, pearl-gray suit, her long hair held prisoner by more than twenty pins, making her look all business. It was only when she grinned that the young girl emerged again.

"This is an unexpected treat. They told me you were waiting for me, but I thought someone made a mistake." She deposited an armload of files onto her desk beside the computer. Research was a bear. "So, where have you been keeping yourself? Or am I not supposed to ask?"

"Ordinarily, you're not," he acknowledged. "But I need your help."

The admission stunned her, but she was quick to recover.

"This is new." She took a seat, perching on the edge of her chair. "Since when does my big brother need anything from me?"

"Not from you, exactly," he amended, habit making him not admit anything directly. "But from the D.A." Hesitating, he framed his words slowly. "I need to bring someone a deal."

Right in front of his eyes, his sister became the A.D.A. "What kind of deal?"

He sighed, still not entirely certain if this was the way to go. Then again no other course was open to him. And all the while, in his mind's eye, he could see Maren. Could see the disappointment in her eyes. Or worse.

"I need to offer someone immunity."

Janelle folded her hands in front of her, her voice patient. It was as if she could sense just how important all this was to him. "In exchange for?"

"The man's help in bringing down a money laundering scheme."

If she was surprised, she didn't show it. Instead she was the picture of a dedicated assistant D.A., sworn to do her duty to uphold the laws of the state. "How much evidence do we have?"

He shook his head, his frustration evident. "Not much. All just circumstantial, really. The one person who talked to us is dead." He saw her eyes widen. "They've been very, very careful."

She seemed to mull over options. "The D.A. has his eye on becoming the governor of this great state in the not too distant future. Will the evidence you hope to get from this man bring down anyone of importance?"

He hedged his words carefully. "It could possibly bring down members of a prominent crime family."

"Just possibly?" she prodded.

Jared gave her what he could. This was still all on a need-to-know basis. "The evidence I need to substantiate anything is in a computer. The only way into that computer is through the accountant. A decent guy."

Still sitting on the edge of her chair, she asked the obvious. "If he's such a decent guy, what's he doing mixed up in this?"

Which was why he'd been wavering about all this. But he had his back against a wall. It wasn't a crime to buy new equipment, wasn't a crime to be in the black when you should have been in the red. Unless the money was coming from investors who stole for a living and were beefing up the prices of the equipment being brought in. And the only way he could hope to find that out was through Joe. Because he'd liked numbers, he'd minored in accounting at college. He knew enough to find inconsistencies. But first he had to get his hands on them.

"That's what I'm trying to find out." Something compelled him to come to Joe's defense, even if his sister didn't know who he was talking about. "You know as well as I do that not everyone's black and white. Sometimes there's some gray."

"Only if you're using bad laundry detergent."

Jared got to his feet. He needed to go in and didn't have much time left. "Janelle, I don't have time to debate this. Can you help me?"

"Just a second." Reaching into her desk drawer, Janelle took out a tape recorder.

Jared's eyes narrowed. Trained to blend in, he didn't like the idea of any kind of recording devices near him. "What's that?"

"What does it look like? It's a tape recorder. I just want you to repeat that last line for me before I go talk to Davidson," she said, mentioning the D.A. by name. Her eyes were shining as she looked at her brother. "Nobody's ever going to believe you asked me to help you unless I have proof. C'mon," she held the recorder up to him. "Say it."

He sighed, then repeated the words she asked for. "Can you help me?"

Janelle depressed the Stop button. The whirling noise ceased. If her grin was any broader, it was in danger of splitting her face.

"Perfect." Depositing the recorder back into her middle drawer, she rose from the desk. "Okay, I'm going to go and beard the lion in his den. You wait right here for me."

Relieved, Jared nodded. They didn't have the deal yet, but if anyone could get it for him, he knew that Janelle could. His sister was like a pit bull once she was let loose.

As she opened the door to leave, Jared called after her. "Janelle?"

She paused, her hand on the knob, and looked over her shoulder. "Yes?"

"Thanks."

She grinned, nodding at her desk. "Remind me to get that on tape, too, when I get back." And then she left the room.

Chapter 13

Less than forty-five minutes later Jared had his deal.

As he drove through the dark streets of Aurora, some fifteen hours later, that same deal weighed heavily on his mind. Janelle had secured a verbal agreement from the district attorney that the offer—immunity in exchange for concrete information leading to the arrest and conviction of the party or parties behind the money laundering transactions—would be placed into writing the moment that Joe agreed to the bargain.

All he needed to do now was to approach Joe. The man had been at the other restaurant all day so he'd had all that time to stew about his next giant step. Talking to Joe. And dropping his cover.

An SUV cut him off, and he had to stomp on the brake to keep from becoming one with the flying vehicle. Jared upbraided himself for not being more alert. He had to stop thinking about the case until he got to Joe's house.

It wasn't confronting Joe that bothered him. It was the look on Maren's face when she finally realized what he'd been doing at the restaurant. Gathering information. Pumping people. Pumping her.

Despite the fact that they were all brothers under the uniform, that he had more than his share of relatives on the force and that his father was the chief of detectives, he knew that the department generally didn't give a rat's rear end about personal repercussions. Lying to Maren had just been part of the job, and all the department cared about was the law. It cared about keeping men who made money off the misery of others from growing richer by posing as respected businessmen. It cared about keeping them from being rewarded because crime wasn't supposed to pay. The fact that there would be an emotional casualty or two, well, those were the breaks. Better an emotional casualty than an actual physical one.

He didn't used to have trouble wrapping his mind around that. He did now.

Jared raced through the next light, tension governing his movements, and he had to force himself to ease up. The last thing he wanted was to complicate things further by getting into an accident. He needed to get this over with. After all, he had signed on to this gig and had a responsibility to see it through.

But he hadn't known Maren when he'd signed on, hadn't known that his life would be forever changed by a smile that lit up his soul as well as every single part of him. Jared shook his head as he turned down an oak-tree-lined road. Never in a million years would he have thought that he would ever find himself in this situation. He'd figured that he was beyond that, immune. That his heart was not for the losing.

A hell of a lot he knew. Not only had he lost his heart, but he'd done it at the worst possible time. Frustrated, powerless to stop what he knew was coming, Jared drove onto Joe's street. A sense of déjà vu slipped over him.

Déjà vu with a difference.

The last time he'd been here, Maren had been in the car with him. A host of possibilities had lain open to him. Now there were only dead ends and darkness. What a difference a few days made, he couldn't help thinking.

He wanted to make a U-turn and go back. But it had to be done. He needed to talk to Joe, needed to know once and for all if this was all just an elaborate wild-goose chase, or if all the signs, all the whispers, were on target. Emil's death made him believe that they were.

But either way, asking for Joe's help was going to "out" him. And most likely make Maren hate him.

With a heart that felt as if it had been forged out of

lead, he pulled his car up beside Joe's in the driveway. The garage was closed. It was past eleven, but there were lights on in the front of the house. He recalled Joe mentioning that he needed little sleep these days, going to bed after midnight and rising in time to "wake the roosters."

Bracing himself for whatever was to come, Jared rang the bell. He heard footsteps on the other side of the door and then saw the door being opened.

"Jared." Joe stared at him as if he'd just popped out of a magic lantern. "This is a surprise." His expression more than a little puzzled, Joe opened the door wider. "Come on in." Closing the door again, he turned to face Jared. He was about to say something when the expression on Jared's face evaporated any and all small talk. "Something wrong, Jared?"

"Yeah, something's wrong," Jared replied quietly. So wrong, he didn't know where to begin now that he was face to face with the man he'd grown to like so much in such a short period of time. Any way you sliced it, there was something wrong. He was either going to insult an honest man or take a chance that a criminal was really honest at heart and could be turned.

There was no other way to do it but to do it. But still, rather than plunge ahead, he hedged a little. Giving Joe the opportunity to fabricate something and cover his tail.

"Joe, have you noticed anything strange going on at the restaurant?"

"Strange?" Joe repeated the word cautiously as he led the way back into his living room. Sitting down in his recliner, he motioned for Jared to take a seat on the sofa.

This wasn't going to work, Jared thought, sitting down. He'd felt more relaxed in a courtroom, being grilled by a defense lawyer. What he needed was to get to the heart of the matter and to see if Joe would meet him halfway.

He took a breath and this time plunged ahead. "Joe, I'm not really who I led you and Maren to believe I was."

A guarded look came over the other man's face. "Could have fooled me." Joe seemed unwilling to hear the confession. And then he smiled. It was a weary smile, as if he had been waiting for this and could now finally put his burden down. "But then, I guess maybe that was the point, wasn't it?" He laughed softly. "You give one hell of a damn good imitation of a chef. Who taught you how to cook?"

"My uncle Andrew." He was getting sidetracked. Jared focused. "My name is Jared Cavanaugh. I'm a detective on the Aurora police force. We're investigating allegations that Rainbow's End is a front for money laundering." He looked at the other man intently. Joe's gaze met his dead-on. He couldn't fathom what was beneath it. "Do you know anything about that?"

Joe took his time answering, but then gave Jared the reply he needed. "I knew all along you weren't trying to access the Internet, even though I told myself you were after you called Maren." The need for deception, for omission, was over. "I left that cell phone on you on purpose to see what you would do. But either way, I had a hunch you were here for a reason and it wasn't to make soufflés."

Things fell into place. "You were the one who hit me from behind and put me in the walk-in." Jared didn't want to believe it, but he had no choice.

Jared looked at the accountant, a man he might have been friends with under different circumstances. A man he still wanted to be friends with. God, but he hated his job sometimes. "Not that I don't appreciate it, Joe, but why didn't you just get rid of me?"

Joe shook his head. "Not my way. I was hoping, if you were spying, just to scare you off. Besides, I wasn't sure you were up to something. When you called Maren instead of the police, I told myself that you were just fooling around on the wrong computer, trying to get on the Internet. Every fourth person seems to be addicted to that these days." He blew out a long, deep breath seeming twice as old as he was. "Guess I was wrong." Silence hung between them for a moment. "So, now what?"

Jared moved forward on the sofa. "I need your help."

The words were clearly not what Joe had expected to hear. "What?"

"I need your help," Jared repeated. Taking a breath, he began to lay it all out for Joe. "My sister is an assistant D.A.—"

Like a man barreling down an incline with no brakes on his vehicle, Joe scrubbed his hands over his face, overwhelmed. "Oh, boy."

Jared was quick to try to allay the other man's fears. "She went to the D.A. for me. I think we got you a deal you can live with."

Resignation turned to confusion. A lifeline suddenly dangled before him where a moment ago there was none. "A deal? What kind of deal?"

"Immunity for your cooperation."

Joe's tone was cautious, disbelieving. "Why would you do that?"

Jared answered as honestly as he could. "Because I can't get the information I need without you and because Maren would never forgive me if you were arrested and taken away to prison."

At the mention of Maren's name, Joe straightened. "She's not part of this," Joe informed him quickly.

Jared didn't know if the man was covering for Maren or not, but he took the words at face value. Because he wanted to believe in her innocence. "But you are."

Joe made no attempt to deny it. "Yeah."

Greed was the undoing of many people, but Joe didn't strike him as someone who was led around by the nose by avarice. Something else had to be at the heart of this. He refused to believe that he'd been so wrong about Joe. "Mind if I ask why?"

The wide shoulders rose and fell in a helpless gesture. "I didn't have a choice."

"Everyone has a choice."

Joe dragged his hand through his salt-and-pepper hair. His expression told Jared he was being naive. "Not with these people." Joe seemed to weigh his words carefully before doling them out, but it was time to bring someone else in. "I found a discrepancy in the accounting. Shepherd found out that I knew."

Jared honed in on the piece of information Joe had just substantiated. "So Shepherd *is* behind this."

Joe looked mildly surprised that Jared had entertained any doubts. "Yes."

"And Rineholdt?" Jared pressed, bringing up the so-called silent partner's name.

Joe laughed without mirth. "There is no Rineholdt. That was the discrepancy I found. Money supposedly coming from him was being forwarded through a series of dummy corporations, all with mob ties. Offshore accounts were involved. It had 'illegal' stamped all over. Shepherd got wind of my 'research' and threatened me. His threats didn't hold much weight until he said he'd kill Maren unless I kept my mouth shut and went along with this. He 'needed' me, too," he added wryly, looking at him. The older man clasped Jared by the wrist, as if to bond him to the promise he was about to extract. "Look, I don't care about myself, but I want your word that you'll use whatever methods you have at your disposal to protect Maren."

"I can take care of myself. I don't need a liar looking out for me."

Both men turned to see Maren walk into the room from the rear of the house. Her eyes blazed as she glared at Jared.

For one of the few times in his life, Jared was caught completely off guard. Maren's car hadn't been parked outside. There was no reason to suppose she was at the house.

On his feet, he stared at her. "What are you doing here?"

When she'd first heard his voice, she'd hurried from the kitchen to greet him. But just as she was about to come around the corner, she'd heard him talking to Joe. Heard him say what he was really doing at the restaurant. She'd hid, listening, growing more and more agitated. And furious.

"Finding out that I'm still the same lousy judge of character I always was." She stood beside Joe, her message clear. She was taking sides.

Jared struggled to collect himself. "Your car's not outside."

"It's in the garage." And lucky for her that it was, she thought. Otherwise she might have continued being fooled. Continued being the idiot. "I just had it detailed and I wanted it to stay clean for at least a day."

Tears threatened to spill but she fought them back. She was babbling about cars when her heart was breaking. And it was all Jared's fault, damn him. She caught hold of her anger. "What the hell do you mean, coming into our lives, spying on us?"

He'd never apologized for what he did before, never felt the need. But these were good people, he thought, and he had deceived them. In their place, he would have been just a furious. And yet, Joe just looked resigned. It was Maren who looked as if she was going to explode.

Could he blame her? They'd made love together. What had to be going through her mind? He gave her the only excuse he could, and it sounded hollow. Flimsy. "It's my job, Maren."

Her eyes widened in disbelief. Sarcasm dripped from her lips. "Oh, well, your *job*. I guess that makes everything all right as long as you were just doing your job." Her eyes narrowed as she gave him a piercing look of disdain. "Isn't that the excuse the SS officers used in World War II? Except they called it 'following orders.'" She got into his face, her voice rising as her temper grew hotter. "Were you just following orders, Jared-if-that-is-your-real-name," she mocked. And then she was shouting at him. "Did you get orders to ruin our lives?"

It was Joe, of all people, who came to his defense, placing his hand gently over his daughter's. "Maren, you're not being fair."

She spun around to stare at Joe. "Oh, *I'm* not being fair? What about him?" She gestured angrily toward Jared, then turned her hurt on Joe. "What about you?"

All her concern came pouring out. He'd kept this from her, living in danger like this, he'd kept it all from her. Why hadn't they just picked up stakes and left? She would have gone with him. She wouldn't have been alive if it hadn't been for him. Didn't he know she'd always be loyal to him no matter what? All she required was that he be honest with her.

But honesty, it seemed, came at a premium these days. "Oh, Papa, how could you put yourself in harm's way like this?"

"Because I didn't want anything happening to you. Without you, Maren, there is nothing." He looked at Jared, "You said you had a deal?"

Jared nodded. He needed to set things in motion to get these people into some kind of protective custody. But he knew that the D.A. wouldn't go for it before he had the information everyone wanted. "Total immunity," he repeated. "We can put you in the witness security program—"

"No, I'm not hiding anymore," Joe said. "Just put these guys away." He pressed his lips together, thinking. "Your sister, she sharp?"

Jared welcomed the momentary respite in a very tense situation. "Any sharper and she'd make you bleed." He added fuel to the argument for compliance. "The D.A. is salivating to make his name on this. We just need some evidence."

"How much do you need?" Joe asked.

Jared was aware that Maren stared at him. His discomfort level rose with every passing moment. "As much as you can give us. The last thirteen years would be good."

Joe nodded. "That's about when Shepherd and his

'invisible partner' took over." Joe had worked at Rainbow's End for the past fifteen years, ever since he and Maren had come to Aurora. "They bought the place out from Eric Svenson." Joe thought back. "Svenson sold out rather abruptly," he recalled. "Looking back, he must have been pressured."

Jared debated giving the other man the information he'd just become privy to as he'd left Janelle's office. "They found Eric Svenson's body stuffed into an eighteen-gallon drum that washed ashore late Monday night."

Joe paled as the words sank in. He looked at Maren. "I'm sorry, baby, I should have never let you come to work here."

As if she could blame him for anything, she thought. It was just her anger over being duped that had had her lashing out before. That and her fear that something could have happened to Papa Joe. She laid her hand on his shoulder. "You didn't know Shepherd had connections to the mob then, did you?" Joe shook his head. "Then you have got nothing to be sorry for." Her eyes frosted over as she turned them toward Jared. "Unlike some people."

She had every right to be angry at him, but he needed to clear things up between them. "Maren—"

Joe looked from his daughter to Jared. "I think you two need to talk this out. I'll give you a minute alone," Joe said, retreating.

"I don't want a minute alone with him," Maren insisted. But Joe walked out of the room anyway. His footsteps faded down the hall.

Jared tried again, but got no further than the first time. When he said her name, Maren whirled around to face him, nothing less than fury in her eyes. Her look forbade him to take another step toward her.

"Was bedding me part of it?"

The question stunned him. "No—"

Again she wouldn't let him finish. "Then I guess that was just a little bonus, a perk for a job convincingly done."

His father had once said he could charm birds out of the trees and into his hands. All that eluded him now. He had no idea how to get Maren to see his side of it. How to make her forgive him. He could only be honest with her.

"Maren, I didn't plan for any of this to happen."

"Oh, you didn't, did you?" Disbelief echoed in her voice. "You didn't 'plan' on this." She fisted her hands at her waist only to keep from swinging them at him. "Was that why you were there at every turn, doing your damnedest to get me to open up to you?"

She was backing him up into a corner, and he did his best to move out of the way. "That was part of the job, yes, but not the rest of it."

She didn't believe him. Would never believe him—or any man again. Even Joe was on shaky grounds after the lie he'd been living. "Draw fine lines, do you? If it 'wasn't part of it' then why did you make love with me?" she demanded.

Though he was gregarious, he kept a part of himself in reserve. It was why he'd never gotten into a full, three-dimensional relationship with a woman. He took a chance and laid himself bare now. Risking it all. "Because if I didn't, I was going to go insane."

The contemptuous look on her face told him he hadn't been successful. "Is that anything like the Twinkies Defense?"

He wanted to take her by the shoulders and shake her. Instead he shoved his hands deep into his pockets and let his own temper flare. "Damn it, Maren, you have to believe me. What happened between us had nothing to do with my assignment."

She pretended to study him with unabashed awe. "Incredible. You can lie without flinching or blinking. That's some talent you've developed."

He was reaching the end of his tether. "Look, you can believe me, or not believe me, but this isn't how I operate. By the time you and I slept together, I knew you had nothing to do with what was going on."

A part of her, she realized in shame, wanted to believe him. But she couldn't.

"Oh? And how did you know?" she demanded hotly, beckoning him on with her hands as if urging him to move forward. "How were you so sure?"

"Because I couldn't have felt the way I did about you if you were guilty. Because I just would have known." He hit his palm against the flat of his stomach. "In my gut, I would have known."

She struggled not to let the expression on his face get to her, not to allow his tone to undermine the anger she was nursing. Kirk had tried to win her back with lies, with protestations of being faithful only to have her catch him with someone else again. Even then, Kirk had felt he had a chance to win her back, that she would succumb to him because of his charm, his looks. The only way she'd truly gotten rid of him was when she'd told him she was carrying his baby. She'd never seen him after that.

Jared made Kirk look like a choirboy.

"Very good, very convincing," she jeered, frantically placing roadblocks between them. Because even now, she wanted to throw herself into his arms and weep. "Too bad I can see through you."

"No," he told her, his voice suddenly deadly calm, "you can't. Because if you could, you'd know that I was telling the truth."

"The truth?" She hooted. "The truth? You've probably been doing this for so long, you wouldn't know the truth if it bit you on the rear," she cried suddenly as he took a step toward her. "Don't come near me, don't touch me." She uttered the warnings tersely, knowing that if he did touch her, she'd break down and she couldn't afford to do that.

Abruptly she opened the hall closet and grabbed her jacket and purse. "I'm going, Papa," she called. "I'll see you at work tomorrow." And then she looked at Jared. "And you, I'll see in hell."

"I doubt it," he murmured to her retreating back. "It wouldn't be a place where you'd be going." But he would, he thought.

Jared saw her falter for a second and knew she'd heard him. The next minute she was gone, holding his heart hostage.

Chapter 14

Jared grimly flipped closed his cell phone. That made a total of five calls to Joe in the last two hours that had gone unanswered. The alarm system within his head went off. Something was wrong.

Without any further hesitation, he left his apartment, got into his car and drove to Joe's house. At ten o'clock at night, the man had to be home. Joe had made a point of laughing about what a homebody he was.

He'd called initially to tell Joe that he was going in tomorrow morning to give the D.A. the disk that Joe had made for him. The disk was a copy of all the accounting information Joe had pulled off both restaurant computers. On it was every monetary transaction the two branches of Rainbow's End had made in the last fifteen years, going back to when Shepherd and the mythical Rineholdt had originally taken over. Davidson, the D.A., had told him he wanted Joe present along with the disk.

Joe couldn't be there if he didn't know.

Maybe he was getting concerned for no reason, Jared told himself, although when he got that itchy feeling at the back of his neck, he was rarely wrong.

Still, playing the odds, he called Maren's cell phone. Maybe the man was with her.

Maren answered on the third ring. "Hi."

He knew the cheery tone he heard would vanish the moment he identified himself. She'd been downright frosty to him all day. Barely civil. Max had let some snide comment drop about there being "trouble in paradise." Little did Max realize that this was going to be his last day.

Jared knew it was going to take time for Maren to work through her anger. At least, he was hoping she'd work through it. Because he wasn't about to let her just drop out of his life no matter what kind of a scum she thought he was now.

"Maren, it's Jared—don't hang up," he ordered, rightly anticipating her next move. "I'm looking for Joe. Is he there with you?" He'd tried to mask his concern.

"No, why? Isn't he home?"

He stifled the impatience building inside him. As he gripped the wheel, he made a sharp right. "He's not answering his phone. Maybe he just—"

There was a dial tone in his ear. Maren had hung up.

He didn't have to guess where she was going. Throwing down the cell phone onto the passenger seat, Jared pressed down harder on the gas.

Guilt and worry haunted him—and something else he wasn't accustomed to besides these formless, unfamiliar feelings for Maren.

Why wasn't Joe answering his phone? Where the hell was he?

The man had refused police protection, saying that would only attract Shepherd's attention. The accountant, who had been exceptionally cool under fire, wanted things to remain "business as usual" until the trap was sprung. He'd slipped Jared the disk less than three hours ago, just before leaving. Something told Jared that he should have overridden the older man's objections and had someone watching him anyway.

Bending several speeding rules and breaking a few others, Jared reached Joe's house just minutes before Maren did. At least something was going in his favor, he thought.

His opinion began to turn as he pulled up at the curb. Joe's car was parked in the driveway. In a New York minute, a sick feeling chewed a hole in the pit of his stomach. He sprinted to the front door. Not wasting any time knocking, he tried the knob. It gave, adding to his uneasiness.

Jared braced himself and walked in.

The house was completely trashed, as if a hurricane

had passed through. Sofa, chairs and cushions were slashed, their guts spewed everywhere. The TV set had been unseated from its stand and lay facedown on the rug, smashed. Pictures had been thrown from walls, their frames broken and crippled.

"Joe, Joe are you here?" he called.

He didn't see him at first.

And then he realized that it wasn't more debris lying on the floor at the center of the chaos. It was Joe. The man lay in a still, crumpled, bloodied heap, discarded like the rest the things in the room.

Jared was instantly on his knees beside the man, unwilling to process what he saw. Unwilling to believe the man was dead. But Joe wasn't moving, wasn't moaning. Wasn't making a sound. Praying, Jared felt the man's throat for signs of a pulse.

At first, there was none, but then he detected something. It was reedy, barely there, but at least there was a slight beat.

Jared pulled out his cell phone. "You're going to be okay, Joe, I promise." Emotion threatened to cut off his voice.

After getting the dispatcher, Jared identified himself and asked for an ambulance. He requested a forensic team, then gave the address.

With a shaky sigh, Jared broke the connection as he looked down at Joe's swollen, bloodied face. He thought of the disk that was locked away in his father's safe at the police station.

"They came here looking for it, didn't they?" Guilt tore out another chunk. Joe's attackers probably assumed the man was dead, and Jared prayed that they weren't ultimately right. Shepherd and the people he was involved with were desperate. Would they go after Maren, too? She'd answered the phone when he'd called her, which meant she was all right. For now.

God, he wished he'd never gotten them involved. Reminding himself of Joe's involvement didn't assuage what he was feeling.

Joe was bleeding too much. The deep red pool around his body grew. Jared tore the bottom of his shirt, using the material to quickly bandage the wound on Joe's forearm. He wanted to temporarily stem the flow of blood until the paramedics arrived.

Squatting next to the man, anointed with Joe's blood on his hands and clothing, he'd never felt so utterly helpless in his life. "Damn it, Joe, why didn't you listen to me and let that policeman hang around? He could have stopped this from happening to you."

"Oh, my God. Oh, my God!"

Jared's head jerked up in time to see Maren cover her mouth with her hands, trying to stifle a scream. The next minute, she was rushing into the house.

"Get away from him." She physically pushed Jared out of the way and knelt beside Joe to take his place. "Haven't you done enough?" She tried to cradle the unconscious man beside her. "Papa, talk to me. It's Maren, please talk to me."

Jared refrained from pulling her away, from attempting to hold and comfort her because he knew it would only agitate her. "Maren, he can't hear you."

"Yes, he can," she insisted fiercely, because to believe otherwise would be to entertain the frightening possibility of Joe's mortality. "He could always hear me. Even when I was away at school and I needed him, somehow, he'd always know and would call me." She bent closer to his head. "Papa?" she whispered, trying not to choke on the tears in her throat.

Sirens pierced the air. Pulling herself together, she sat upright.

"I called the paramedics," Jared said as the sirens came closer. "There's a pulse—"

The fire in her eyes warned him off. "No thanks to you," she snapped. "We were doing just fine until you came along." Her heart hadn't been broken and Papa Joe hadn't been beaten to a pulp. She'd never forgive him for that. Never.

"He'll pay for this, Maren," Jared told her, his voice low, steely, as he made the promise. "I swear Shepherd will pay for this."

Maren didn't even acknowledge that she'd heard him. She held Joe's hand in both of hers and rocked back and forth.

Paramedics appeared in the doorway, a gurney between them. Jared waved the men in. The duo appeared bewildered by the beating that apparently had taken place.

The younger of the two paramedics squatted down. "Jeez, what the hell happened to this guy?"

Coming around, Maren looked accusingly at Jared. "Someone obviously found out he was talking to the police and tried to kill him." She felt tears stinging her eyes, tears of anger, of fear and helplessness. She blinked them back. There'd be time for tears later. Right now she needed to stay strong for Joe.

Doing what they could for Joe, the two paramedics gently placed the unconscious man on the gurney. Aurora General was the closest hospital; they were taking Joe there.

Jared was torn. He wanted to go with Maren. To be there for her even though she hated his guts right now. And to be there for Joe because, no matter what anyone said to the contrary, he felt it was ultimately his fault that the man had been beaten like this. He should have placed him in protective custody immediately instead of trying to play things out a little longer.

But his duty was clearly outlined. He caught Maren's arm as she began to leave. The look in her eyes almost made him back away. It intensified his guilt.

"Look, I've got to stay here and wait for the forensic team. Call me the minute you know something," he instructed her.

Jerking her arm away from his grasp, she squared her shoulders. "A hell of a lot you care." She practically spat the words at him.

"Yes," he retorted, his own temper snapping under

the weight of what he was enduring, both internally and externally. "I do care. I was the one who wanted him to have police protection."

"You were the one who got him into this in the first place."

Maren's words hung in the air as she walked out behind the paramedics.

She'd held Joe's limp hand in hers all the way to the hospital, talking to him. Assuring him that he was going to be fine. She forced every single word out past the huge lump in her throat.

The emergency room physician had been guarded but optimistic in his prognosis, saying that the wounds actually looked worse than they were. In the pink of health, Joe apparently had excellent stamina and would pull through. The same words were uttered by the surgeon who came to talk to her once Joe was out of surgery and in the recovery room.

In his early sixties, the physician seemed well experienced and justifiably pleased.

"We had to remove his spleen, but we've stopped the internal bleeding and everything looks good. Several of his organs were bruised, but nothing fatal," he added quickly. "He's going to be a very sore man for some time to come, but there's no reason to believe he won't make a full recovery. He was very lucky you found him when you did."

She nodded. If not for Jared's call, she wouldn't have

gone to see Joe. And if neither of them had gone to his house, Joe could very well have bled to death.

She couldn't curtail the shiver that seized her.

The look in the surgeon's eye was one of pure kindness. "Your father's probably not going to wake up for another twelve, fifteen hours, if not more. We can call you if there's any change," he promised. "We have your home and cell phone numbers. Why don't you go home and get some rest?"

Maren nodded, knowing the doctor meant well. She was going to go home all right, but she wouldn't sleep a wink.

The weapon felt cool in her hand. Cool and hard and up to the job.

She hadn't held it for a long time now.

Now, as before, the gun resided deep in Joe's closet. It was a holdover from the days when they'd lived in L.A. in a less than desirable neighborhood. Joe had worked like a dog to scrape together enough money to get them out of there. When they'd moved, the weapon had come with them.

Burrowing into the depths of her father's closet, exploring the way kids did, she had uncovered the gun when she was a few weeks shy of fourteen. As with everything, she'd taken the matter to Joe.

Rather than lecture her about guns or about invading someone's privacy, Joe told her that he would stay out of her closet if she'd stay out of his. Sealing the bargain with a handshake, he'd then taken her to a gun range. He'd taught her how to use the weapon if she should ever need to defend herself. He'd taught her how to respect its power and never to abuse it.

By the time she'd stopped going to the range, she could shoot the wings off a fly at fifty feet.

It wasn't a fly she was after tonight.

After putting in a fresh clip, she tucked the gun into her purse. Logically she knew she should leave this up to Jared, the way he'd told her. But anger overruled logic. Shepherd's men could have killed Joe. They'd left him for dead, of that she was certain.

She'd put up with the man's barely veiled lewd remarks, his one-step-away-from-harassment actions. But this was a whole different ballgame. He wasn't going to get away with it.

The computer in Joe's study was her next stop. She'd learned it had a program that couldn't be found in any of the usual software stores. The kind that gave hackers a rush.

Among the things it could do was allow a few well-placed series of keystrokes to compromise the security systems of the average business and home. Because she enjoyed challenging herself, Maren knew her way around the program, though she had never put it to any use, other than to disable and enable the security code at the restaurant. She'd done that just to see if the program would work. It did.

There was one more thing she had to do before she

was ready. It didn't take long. Once she locked up the house, she got into her car. And drove to Shepherd's house.

Jared stuck around Joe's house as long as he was needed. But the moment the CSI unit leader told him that they would take over, Jared was back inside his car.

Maren hadn't called him from the hospital and that left a sick feeling in his gut. But she'd made it clear that she wanted no part of him, so for now, he'd leave her alone and hope for the best.

Besides, he had other business to tend to.

The weapon he'd thought to take with him, his backup gun that he normally wore strapped to his calf, was still locked in his glove compartment. He unlocked it and took it out. Rather than holster it, he placed it next to him on the seat. It rode shotgun as he turned his vehicle in the direction of Shepherd's house.

There was little doubt in his mind that the man knew when to call it quits. By now Shepherd had to know what had happened, that his money laundering involvement was on the verge of being exposed. There was no other reason for the savage attack on Joe.

Whether Shepherd was still looking for the disk or had assumed that it had already changed hands was anyone's guess. But the man hadn't gotten this far in his life by being stupid. Dollars to doughnuts, Shepherd had a contingency plan. More than likely, it involved disappearing.

Jared zoomed through a light. With luck Shepherd would stop at his house to get some traveling money as well as the account numbers to his offshore bank accounts. Jared wasn't a betting man, but it seemed like a sure thing that Shepherd would be preparing to leave the country.

Jared had already called for backup. His plan was to stall Shepherd any way he could until they arrived. If that meant boldly strolling onto Shepherd's compound and asking to talk to the man himself, so be it. He was up to it on adrenaline alone.

As he drove, an idea came to him, making plausible the stalling tactic he wanted to implement. He could try to make Shepherd believe that he still had the disk, locked in a safe place and that he was willing to trade it for a cut of the business. He could lie convincingly enough to plant doubts in Shepherd's head. At least long enough until help arrived.

Pulling up in front of the towering white gates in front of Warren Shepherd's estate, Jared leaned out and pressed the buzzer located on the side of the brick post. He waited, but there was no response. Pressing it again, he realized that though he listened, he didn't hear the buzzer make any noise.

Puzzled, he got out of the car and tried the gates. After tugging on them, they parted easily enough, as if no current flowed through them to prohibit any unwanted visits.

That itchy feeling at the back of his neck intensified. He didn't like this.

Looking around, he expected to see anything from bodyguards to Ninja warriors descending on him. But nothing moved. Even the guard dogs that Shepherd was rumored to have didn't put in an appearance.

Was he already gone?

Jared left his car where it was and went the rest of the way to the estate-like house on foot. Even from a distance, he could see that there were lights on in every window of the ground floor of the three-storied sprawling house. Had the rats left the sinking ship? Or was there some kind of trap waiting for him on the other side of the front door?

Or, had Rosetti gotten wind of what had gone down and decided, childhood friendship notwithstanding, to burn his bridges behind him, cut his losses and get rid of Shepherd?

The myth that there was honor among thieves was just that, a myth.

Like the gates at the edge of the grounds, the front door was unlocked. *Something is wrong here,* a voice echoed inside his head. Still, he'd come too far to turn back. Stealthily, Jared entered and immediately heard raised voices coming from somewhere inside the house. Listening, he made out Shepherd's. There was a note of fear in it.

"You're not going to get away with this, bitch."

"I don't want to get away with it. I just want to see you dead. But first I want to see you mangled and bleeding on the floor, just the way you left Joe."

Oh, God, it was Maren. He'd recognized the voice the moment she'd said the first word. Adrenaline shot through him as he hurried toward the source of the voices.

As he made his way, he remained alert against one of Shepherd's henchmen springing out at him from some corner of the house. But then it occurred to him that if there were any of his people around, they would have been trying to get the drop on Maren. It was obvious from what he was hearing that she had gotten the upper hand on Shepherd.

He tried not to think what that implied.

"I didn't do anything to your old man," Shepherd said, the tremor in his voice escalating.

Maren's tone was steely, unshakable—and unlike anything he'd heard coming from her before, even when she was angry with him.

"Maybe not personally, but you watched. I know you watched, you sick son of a bitch. The only reason Papa Joe stayed at Rainbow's End was because he was afraid of what you'd do to me if he tried to leave. But that's your speed, isn't it, Shepherd? Threatening women you think are defenseless." Jared thought he heard the sound of a gun being cocked. "Well, I'm not defenseless now, am I?"

"Please, Maren, we can work something out."

"I don't think so."

Jared walked into the room to see that Maren had Shepherd on his knees. The man's hands were clasped behind his head as he stared up at her fearfully.

The gun in her hand was aimed at Shepherd's chest.

Chapter 15

Jared judged that she was in a very dangerous state of mind. He'd been in situations like this before, where perfectly law-abiding citizens had been pushed too far and reacted on impulse. But the confidence with which Maren held her gun told him that she hadn't just borrowed someone's weapon, she knew how to use it. No overripe anxiety caused her hands to shake. On the contrary, they were steadier than rocks on the ground.

He needed to keep her from making a fatal mistake. His eyes on both her and the gun she was pointing, he took a tentative step forward.

"Maren, I didn't expect to find you here." Jared kept his tone calm, friendly.

She knew he was going to get here sooner or later.

If he was any kind of a cop, conclusions would have brought him here. By the sound of it, he was alone. She refused to take her eyes off the trembling coward in front of her. "Life's full of little surprises."

Jared nodded, taking his time, wanting nothing to set her off. "That's a fact."

Only Shepherd gave way to hysteria. His eyes were like two brown marbles as they looked from the weapon to Jared and then back again. "What the hell is this, some kind of freakin' sitcom? Take the gun away from her. The crazy idiot is going to shoot me."

Jared took a breath along with another step. He stopped when she cast a warning glance in his direction before looking back at Shepherd.

"Are you?" Jared asked.

She never flinched. The temptation of payback was tremendous. If she began to think about the way Joe had looked when she'd walked into the house… "I'm seriously considering it."

"You don't want to do that, Maren."

The calm, authoritative note in his voice got under her skin. Just who the hell did Jared think he was? "And just how would you know what I would or wouldn't want to do?"

The tightrope beneath his feet was taut. He trod across it very cautiously, not a hundred percent sure what would set her off. "Haven't a clue, Maren, just talking cause and effect here. You kill him, we wind up losing a possible witness against Rosetti."

Shaking, Shepherd stared at him in disbelief. "You think I'm crazy?" he cried, his face paling. "Rosetti'll have me killed."

He took another half step in Maren's direction, pretending to think over Shepherd's protest. "I don't really see much difference in your situation, Shepherd. She squeezes that trigger, you're dead now. If the D.A. thinks you have something to offer, maybe he'll put you in the witness security program. You won't live the lavish lifestyle you've been living, but you'd live." Rather than move toward Maren, he surprised them both by going toward Shepherd instead. If worse came to worst, he figured he could shield the man with his own body. Shepherd was an integral factor in the case. "How about it, Shepherd, what'll it be? The lady or the D.A.?"

"Aren't you forgetting something?" When he turned to look at her, Maren's eyes indicated the gun she was holding.

"No, I'm not forgetting something," Jared responded as calm as Shepherd was agitated. "But I'm banking on the fact that you wouldn't be able to kill a man in cold blood."

Maybe he did get points for knowing her, she thought. But she didn't want Shepherd to doubt that she was a threat. Trying to negate any confidence that might be budding, she gestured at Shepherd with her gun barrel and had the pleasure of watching him quake. "How about you? Are you willing to bank on it?"

The man's terror quickly overrode any false bravado

he might have had at his disposal. He turned toward Jared. "Okay, okay, I'll talk to the D.A. Just get this lunatic away from me."

"Talk to the D.A. about what?" Maren persisted.

"That I had your old man beaten because he made copies of the records."

"And Joe was never a willing accomplice, was he?" she continued. When the other man didn't answer quickly enough, she raised the gun barrel to his head.

"No, no, he wasn't," Shepherd cried. "I made him help us by telling him I'd have you killed if he did. You satisfied now?" Shepherd railed, spitting as he asked the question.

Maren smiled as she reached into her pocket with her other hand. And took out a tape recorder. She shut it off. "I am now. I got what I came for."

For the second time that evening, Jared heard the whine of distant sirens pierce the darkness. Backup was arriving, he thought. They'd be here within the next five minutes if not less.

"You weren't going to kill him, were you?" Jared asked as he put out his hand for her gun.

After a moment she surrendered the weapon. "I couldn't honestly tell you. It was touch-and-go for a while," she admitted. "But I knew I had to get him to clear Papa Joe's name."

Jared kept his own weapon trained on Shepherd in case the man had any ideas about getting away. "That's my girl."

"No," she said firmly, holding on to independence with both hands, "I'm not." Maren sighed inwardly. It was over. Secretly she'd hoped that Shepherd would attempt to lunge at her while she'd held the gun on him, giving her an excellent excuse to shoot him. But the pompous man in the three-thousand-dollar suits had sank down to his knees almost instantly. Just a coward at heart.

Jared shoved the weapon she'd just given him into the back of his waistband. He looked around. The place was too empty, too eerie.

"Where is everyone?" he wanted to know.

"Gone," she told him. She'd gotten the story from Shepherd at gunpoint. "Once they'd realized that they were all just walking liabilities, that the evidence would probably put them behind bars for a very long time and that Rosetti would more than likely get rid of Shepherd rather than risk having him talk, they deserted the kingpin here so fast you couldn't see them for the dust." Sarcasm and satisfaction dripped from her voice. If she couldn't kill him, at least she could have the pleasure of watching his kingdom fall. "Joe not only detailed the monetary transactions, along with a fake set of books, he also kept a journal online of the people involved. That's why Shepherd sent his men to get the disk from him."

But all that presupposed a knowledge of Joe's enlistment by the D.A. Only the three of them, plus Janelle and Davidson knew about that part. He hadn't even told his superior about it. He refused to mentally accuse anyone of leaking the information. He looked at Maren. "How did they know?"

Maren shook her head. In the background, the squad cars had arrived. The sirens had ceased their threatening song. "I don't know."

But there was one man in the room who did. Jared cocked his weapon, pointing it straight at the kneeling man. "Shepherd?"

Shepherd scowled. "Max."

Maren was stunned. Wasn't anyone who they said they were? "Max is in on this, too?"

"That jerk?" Shepherd hooted contemptuously. "Hell, no." He looked at Jared because he held the weapon. "He just let it slip that you were sniffing around Maren and that Joe was burning the midnight oil in the office. Since there was no reason for any extra input on that double-crosser's part, I got suspicious." He shook his head, obviously remembering what had gone down a few short hours ago. "Tough guy. Wouldn't tell me what he was doing, but I knew. I knew he had to have copied the files. Footprints on the program gave him up. The last thing that old guy said to me was, 'Go to hell.'"

Fury crowded her all over again. "You bastard!"

Shepherd's raised hands went up higher. "I was strictly there as an observer," he cried, panic entering his voice. He swung his head around to look at Jared. "I never touched the guy."

Jared saw the look in Maren's eyes and knew what

she was thinking. She wished she had the gun back. But the house was filling up with detectives.

"Hell, is this thing all wrapped up already?"

Jared turned at the sound of the familiar, disappointed voice to see his younger brother Troy walk into the room, followed by a number of uniformed patrolman.

Troy jerked a thumb behind him toward the opened door. "Casey has the S.W.A.T. team all ready to go outside," he said, referring to the sergeant in charge of the sharpshooters.

"Nothing to swat," Jared responded dryly. He nodded at the man who was still on his knees. "You want to take over, Troy? I'm about done for the day."

A grin played on Troy's face. There was nothing he liked better than bringing in the bad guys.

"You always did take the easy way out, big brother." He indicated the man about to be taken into custody. "This Shepherd?"

Jared nodded. "He says he has an earful for the D.A. And if he doesn't feel like talking, we've got most of it on tape, thanks to Maren here."

Producing handcuffs, Troy took Shepherd by the arm and jerked him up to his feet. "Ready to sing?" he asked the man. He spun Shepherd around so that he could handcuff his wrists behind him.

"Hold it." Stepping forward, Jared took the handcuffs from his brother. He held them up in front of Maren. "You want to do the honors?"

Her surprise faded, to be replaced by pleasure. "I'd love to," Maren replied with relish. She snapped the cuffs on one at a time. "Although it's still won't compare to shooting him and watching him bleed out."

"In the long run, this'll be worse." Giving the cuffs a tug to make certain they were secure, he pushed Shepherd toward his brother. "And I won't have to bake you a cake with a file in it. I'm not much at baking," Jared confided.

"He isn't," Troy agreed, putting in his two cents. He beckoned one of the uniformed policeman over. "Take this scum down to the station."

Jared suddenly felt tired and wired at the same time. He looked at Maren before telling Troy, "I'll be in in the morning to do the paperwork."

"I'll be sure to have the confetti for the ticker tape parade ready," Troy quipped before he got down to the business of securing the area.

Crossing to Maren, Jared second-guessed where she would go from here. It wasn't hard. "Can I take you back to the hospital?"

She didn't know if she was ready to be with this man. She was still nursing her anger. It might take a while to work her way through that. Besides, there was the problem of logistics to address. "I drove my own car, remember?"

Apparently he'd already taken that fact into account before making his offer. "I can have one of the uniforms drive it over to your place."

She shook her head. The man was still smooth, even under life-and-death circumstances. Smooth with a dark center. Like black velvet. "Like I said before, you've got an answer for everything, don't you?"

"Not everything," he allowed. "I don't have an answer for how long it's going to take you to forgive me."

Even as he said it, she knew that she was more than half leaning his way. Still, she couldn't make it too easy for him. "What makes you think I'll forgive you?"

There were too many people around. He wanted to be alone with her. Taking her by the arm, Jared guided her outside the house.

That she let him gave him hope.

The night was crisp, clear. He should have stopped for her jacket, but he was too intent on clearing this up. Maybe if she was cold, she'd see things his way faster. "Because I'm an optimist at heart."

So had she been. Once. But that was before all her illusions had been shattered. "There's optimist, and then there's fool. Believe me—" a touch of cynicism entered her voice "—I know all about that."

"You're not a fool, Maren."

"Aren't I?" She raised her chin. The fight was still in her eyes. "I fell in love with someone who didn't even exist."

"The name didn't exist. At least, not the last name. But the man did." Unable to stop himself, he lightly touched her cheek. Wanting to caress it. For now, he held himself in check. "The man does."

She glanced toward the open door and saw Troy pass by inside. The detective had called him "big brother." "You really have two brothers and a sister?" she asked.

His lips quirked in a grin. "Got the scars to prove it." Pushing up his sleeve, he showed her the faintest discoloration along the inside of his forearm. "That's where Janelle bit me when she couldn't get out of a wrestling hold I had on her when we were kids." He rolled his sleeve back down. "I've also got a ton of cousins if you're interested in those," he offered. "They can be yours for the asking."

She raised an eyebrow. "You're selling them?"

"Actually," he corrected, "I'm offering them. In exchange."

"In exchange for what?"

This time he did caress her cheek. He wanted this to be behind them. But she deserved to work this out of her system at her own pace.

"You."

Was he asking her to forget what happened? To start fresh? "I don't understand."

To have a better foundation for his argument, he backtracked. "You just said you fell in love with me."

"With Jared Stevens," she clarified. Besides, it wasn't really love she'd left, just loneliness, Maren silently insisted. Loneliness made you do strange things. "And I got confused."

"I didn't." He traced the outline of her lips with his thumb. She didn't pull away immediately, and he grew more hopeful. "Maybe for the first time in my life, everything's really clear to me."

She couldn't trust her emotions. They only served to mix her up and to muddy the water. "Well, it isn't clear to me. I don't know who or what you are. And don't give me any of that garbage about 'what you see is what you get.' It isn't."

But he had a different opinion. A part of him was in every character he became. And never more so than this last time. If only because, at first, he tried to keep his facts straight. And then, because every lie he'd told her had hurt.

"It is when you come right down to it. No matter who I play, I'm still me. I'm still the guy who wasn't looking to fall in love, who thought that love was a nice fringe benefit to life but that it only complicated things." He raised her chin with his finger, forcing her to look at him when she looked away. "I was right about that, you know. It does complicate things. Because now all I can do is think about you."

"They teach you those lines at the police academy?"

"Nobody taught me what I'm saying now. I had to learn that for myself. And they come from the bottom of my heart." He took her hands in his, willing her to believe him. "Like I was saying, I wasn't looking to fall in love, but I did. Hard. With you," he added in case she was going to be flippant and ask to know who the object of his affections was. "And until just a few minutes ago, I didn't know what I was going to do about it."

She looked at him skeptically. Knowing she was losing the battle but trying desperately to still win it. "But now you know."

"Now I know," he repeated.

Damn, he was good. She could feel her knees melting even though she kept telling herself he was lying. "And it came to you when? When you saw me holding a gun on Shepherd?"

"Actually, yes."

Without all the information, she drew the only conclusion she could. "Are you into kinky things?"

"No," he laughed. "Only into you." And then he grew serious. "What came to me was the thought of spending the rest of my life without you if you pulled that trigger. What came to me was that I was willing to lie, to ignore what had happened, just to keep you safe. I've never been willing to do that before."

She stared at him. He'd almost had her. But he'd blown it. The man lied by profession. "Yeah, sure."

"I don't mean when it came to setting up an undercover operation, I mean where it counts. On the right side of the law." Without realizing it, he placed her hand over his heart. So she could feel it beating. For her. "I've never compromised what I pledged to uphold and defend."

"But you were willing to do that for me."

His eyes never left her face as he tried to find some sign that told him he was, if not home safe, at least close to it. "Yes."

"Why?" she persisted.

"You really don't have a very long attention span, do you?"

He took her into his arms. She was cold. So was he. But there were ways to fix that. And then he realized that she wasn't struggling to get free. She was listening to him. It was going to be all right.

If he was careful.

"Because I love you," he told her. Emotion threatened to choke him. He'd never felt like this before because nothing had ever mattered this much before. "Maren, I want you to be my wife."

"For a sting operation."

"No, damn it." Didn't she understand? Or was she just trying to torture him because she thought he deserved it. "Forever."

She wanted to fling herself into his arms. Wanted to have him kiss her until she was senseless again. But she needed to find her way to trusting him again. It was a shaky, narrow path. "How do I know that this isn't just another fabrication?"

"You can hook me up to a lie detector if you'd like."

She cocked her head, as if honestly studying his face. "I hear there are ways to beat that."

"I never lied to you where it counted, Maren." He went over just a couple of things he'd told her. "I can cook. It was my uncle who taught me. He just happens to be the chief of police, that's all."

He'd never mentioned what his uncle had done for a living. She'd just assumed it was cooking because he'd let her. "So you're guilty of the sin of omission, as well."

He pressed a kiss to her forehead. God, but he wanted her. But he couldn't hurry this. He'd lose her if he did. "I'll be guilty of whatever you want me to be, as long as you realize that I'm guilty of loving you and that I want you to marry me."

She looked at him for a long moment. "If I marry you, I want to hear all the details."

His eyebrows pulled together in momentary confusions. "Details?"

"Details of the rest of your life." She loved learning about people. And none so much as Jared. "What I have is very sketchy."

"If you marry me, you'll *be* the rest of my life."

She looked up at him, threading her arms around his neck. She was a goner and she knew it. There was no use in pretending otherwise. "You still have all the answers, don't you?"

He framed her face with his hands. "All but the most important one."

She smiled then and it went straight to his gut. "You know, Papa Joe likes you."

"Papa Joe has excellent taste." The air left his lungs. He'd never proposed before, never wanted to propose before. Never wanted anything so much in his life. "So is it yes?"

"Of course it's yes, you big dope. I love you. Or haven't you noticed?"

Framing her face between his hands, he kissed her then, kissed her like a man who had finally found the path that would take his soul out of darkness and into the light. Kissed her like a man who intended to spend a great deal of time at this pastime and wanted to be sure he got it right each and every time.

Hoots and applause caused them to move apart. When he looked, Troy was peering out of the house and giving him the high sign. He moved her out of the way.

"How's Joe doing?" He realized he hadn't asked her.

Maren smiled. "Doctor says he's going to pull through."

"Great. Let's go tell Joe you said yes."

He couldn't have said anything that would have warmed her heart more if he tried.

* * * * *

Don't miss Marie Ferrarella's next romance,
HER GOOD FORTUNE,
from Silhouette Special Edition,
available February 2005!

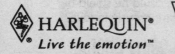

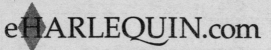

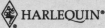

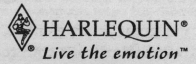

Silhouette®

COMING NEXT MONTH

#1345 PROTECTING THE PRINCESS—Carla Cassidy
Wild West Bodyguards

Bodyguard Tanner West knew Princess Anna Johansson was trouble the second she demanded his help. He could protect the spoiled royal from the rebels trying to kill her, but he didn't have to like her. Yet, despite their clashes, Tanner couldn't deny his attraction to Anna. He'd begun the job protecting a princess, but when had it become personal?

#1346 EXPLOSIVE ALLIANCE—Catherine Mann
Wingmen Warriors

Bo Rokowsky's guilt-ridden dreams had been haunted by Paige Haugen and the part he'd played in her husband's death. Now the air force captain just wanted to check up on the single mother, but he was surprised by the desire she aroused in him. And when Paige began receiving threats, Bo knew he would risk everything to keep her safe.

#1347 STOLEN MEMORY—Virginia Kantra
Trouble in Eden

Reclusive millionaire inventor Simon Ford woke up on the floor of his lab with a case of amnesia, a missing fortune in rubies and a lot of questions. Could he trust by-the-book cop Laura Baker to pose as his girlfriend and help him solve the mystery? Even when her father became their number one suspect…?

#1348 TRULY, MADLY, DANGEROUSLY—
Linda Winstead Jones
Last Chance Heroes

Sadie Harlow's arrival in her small Alabama hometown shouldn't have created a stir, but the two murders that coincided with it sure did. Not everyone thought it was just a coincidence, and Sadie suddenly found herself a suspect. Luckily, her teenage crush, deputy sheriff Truman McCain, believed in her innocence. Would he be able to prove it before the killer struck again?

#1349 STRANGER IN HER ARMS—Lorna Michaels

Christy Matthews had gone on vacation to recover from her divorce, but a sexy amnesiac wasn't exactly the distraction she was looking for. And although he was the first man in a long time to stir her heart, it soon became clear that someone wanted Christy's mysterious guest dead—because only his elusive memory held the key to a crime….

#1350 WARRIOR WITHOUT A CAUSE—Nancy Gideon

Aloof mercenary trainer Jack Chaney was the last person straight-arrow legal assistant Tessa D'Angelo would turn to for help…if her life weren't in danger. She knew her father was innocent of the crimes he'd been accused of, but if she wanted to live long enough to clear his name, she would need to put herself in Jack's hands.

SIMCNM010